D1003978

XL 52X

LITTLE MALCOLM
AND HIS STRUGGLE
AGAINST THE EUNUCHS

Little Malcolm and his Struggle against the Eunuchs

DAVID HALLIWELL

FABER AND FABER
24 Russell Square
London

First published in 1967
by Faber and Faber Limited
24 Russell Square London WC1
Reprinted 1969
Printed in Great Britain by
Latimer Trend & Co Ltd Whitstable
All rights reserved

© *1966 by David Halliwell*

SBN (Paper edition) 571 08167 3
SBN (Cloth edition) 571 08101 0

All rights in this play are reserved by the Proprietor.
All applications for professional and amateur rights
should be addressed to Peter Crouch Ltd,
18 Soho Square, London, W1

CONDITION OF SALE

This book is sold subject to the condition that it shall not, by way
of trade or otherwise, be lent, re-sold, hired out or otherwise
circulated without the publisher's prior consent in any form of
binding or cover other than that in which it is published and with-
out a similar condition including this condition being imposed on
the subsequent purchaser.

CHARACTERS

MALCOLM SCRAWDYKE
JOHN "WICK" BLAGDEN
IRWIN INGHAM
DENNIS CHARLES NIPPLE
ANN GEDGE

The first performance of *Little Malcolm and His Struggle Against the Eunuchs* was given at the Unity Theatre, London, on 30th March 1965. It was presented by Dramagraph and the cast was as follows:

Malcolm Scrawdyke	DAVID HALLIWELL
Irwin Ingham	MICHAEL CADMAN
John "Wick" Blagden	PHILIP MARTIN
Dennis Charles Nipple	RON CREAM
Ann Gedge	JULIAN BURBURY

Directed and Designed by MIKE LEIGH
Stage Manager: MO RACE
Assistant Stage Manager: ANNE MARIE BOXALL

The play was subsequently presented by Michael Codron at the Gaiety Theatre, Dublin, for the Dublin Theatre Festival in September 1965; and the first performance at the Garrick Theatre, London, was given on 3rd February 1966. The latter was directed by Patrick Dromgoole and designed by Timothy O'Brien. The cast was as follows:

Malcolm Scrawdyke	JOHN HURT
Ingham	RODNEY BEWES
Wick	KENNETH COLLEY
Nipple	TIM PREECE
Ann	SUSAN ASHWORTH

The anthem, *Laudation*, referred to on p. 79, is recorded on Southern Record Company, No. MQ 665. This is a non-commercial record obtainable from Stagesound Limited, 11 King Street, London, W.C.2.

SCENE 1

Light slowly comes up on the studio, 3A Commercial Chambers. A grey, wan, wintry light. The room is large and bleak. Upstage is a large deep window. The walls are drab although paint of different colours has been daubed on parts of them. Where there is no paint the colour is a dirty, dingy grey-brown. The floor is of bare grey planks. An upstage recess contains a sink. In the stage left wall is a door, and more or less opposite it, in a shallow chimney breast, is a very small gas fire and nearby a gas ring.

Over towards the door there is a single bed covered in scruffy blankets. A couple of easels stand in the room, on one of which there is a largish, unfinished, self portrait of SCRAW-DYKE. *There is a rickety table. There are two nondescript wooden chairs, a battered armchair, a wooden chair with arms and a high back.* SCRAWDYKE'S CHAIR. *A couple of old tea chests, a large solid old radio cabinet, and a dustbin. There is a record player on the table and a tape recorder somewhere about. To one side there is a large drum with Paramount Jazz Band roughly lettered on it. Paintings on pieces of hardboard are stacked untidily around the room and crockery, records, books, paper and painting gear are littered about in every direction.*

The general atmosphere is empty, squalid, damp and cold.
MALCOLM SCRAWDYKE, *a man of twenty-five, with long hair and a beard, is sitting up in the bed, leaning back against the end, with the clothes pulled up around him. He looks balefully out at the scene.*

SCRAWDYKE: Eeeeeeeergh! Toh. . . . Faah. . . . Get up.
(*He doesn't move.*)
Come on get up!
(*Doesn't move.*)
Must be around two. Been lyin' 'ere an
hour. Got t' get up. A'm starvin'. Look it's
no use just theorisin' about getting up. It's
the act 'at counts. Just a matter of makin'
the decision. Exercise the will. The will!
A'll count up t'five an' then the single
decisive act. Right now. One . . . two . . .
three . . . four . . . five.
(*Doesn't move.*)
Aaaargh! What is it determines the actual
moment when—A mean A alwas do get
up. Always manage it some'ow. What is it
decides? 'Idden factor. Air currents?
Vibrations? Oh 'oo the 'ell—'Ow many
times 'ave I been through all this without it
ever makin' me get up when A say A will!
The thing is t' creep up on y'self, tek y'self
by surprise. Don't think. Suddenly. O.K.
Now!
(*Doesn't move.*)
Blast! All right. Now!
(*This time he leaps out of bed. He is
wearing a raggy black sweater, shirt and
dark, scruffy jeans. He grabs a baggy,
grubby jacket, puts it on.*)
Done it! Done it! Done it! Self-mastery
that's—Ooo 't's cold! Oooooooots! Where's
me—
(*Grabs large black overcoat off bed and
scrambles into it.*)
Aaah! Get it on yes what a life. Ugh.
What a marvellous life for a man like me.

12

(Puts shoes on. He goes to the gas-fire and turns the tap. No gas.)

Fah!

(Searches through pockets.)

Tanner—'a'penny—what's—kopek! What the bloody use is—Oh no shillin'! No gas! No 'eat! 'Ave t' wait till those bastards get up 'ere. Where are they?

(Goes and looks out of window.)

Snow! January 1st. New Year's Day. What a— Put y' mark on this one Malcolm, put y' mark on this one.

(Turns back into room.)

Fag.

(Fumbles one out.)

Give y' the shits first one but—

(Lights it.)

He could get out of bed at two o'clock, light up a fag, an' smoke it, just like that. What a man!

(Pacing around.)

Still A 'aven't started off too badly. Stirred up things down there. An' tonight's the night. 'Ow 'm I goin' to 'andle it? Won't be easy. But I've got t' really make that breakthrough. I know what I'm like but— This time, this time. Don't strain, take it easy. After all I know Ann's int'rested. She asked me. She asked me! That's a salient fact t' keep y'r sights on. All these months of scrapin' up excuses t' talk to 'er finally paid off.

"The's a film at the Empire A'd like t' see, what about . . ." No not "What about—" "Would you". Yes. "Would you." P'raps it's only the picture she's in'rested in. Oh

13

don't be— Remember that tone. Yes this's
my chance. Just take it easy.
Where the 'ell are they? Wonder what's
goin' on down there? Chucked me out the
bastard. Just for 'avin a drag. No it
wasn't— Culmination of five years arsin'
around. Surprised 'e let me go on so long.
Spent 'alf me bloody time down there
sittin' in 'is room bein' given a last chance.
If our positions 'ad been reversed I
wouldn't 'ave tolerated 'im so long. "The
first day back, Scrawdyke, and I catch you
in a petty infraction. You never learn do
you? Well this's the straw that breaks the
camel's back. I'm going to start the New
Year with a clean sweep. I'm kicking you
out, Scrawdyke! That comes as a shock to
you doesn't it?" Well 'e was right, I never
thought 'e'd do it. Why did I go there for
a drag, near 'is door? That was a mistake.
'E's always touchy first few days back. I
should'a' kept out of 'is way. Still I don't
care, I wasn't goin' anywhere down there, I
wouldn't 'ave passed Finals.
Fuck! Allard thinks e's finished me! But
'e's not 'eard the last. You may 'ave the
first word, the second word, the third word
an' the 'undred an' fifteenth word but I
will 'ave the last word! What am A goin' t'
do? Well—I'll make more trouble away
from that place 'an I ever did inside it.
Manipulatin' power from exile. Yeh I like
that. Rule from afar, the gaunt, 'aggard,
ghostlike exile, supposedly finished,
forgotten. But all the time an unseen
presence hauntin' from afar, pullin' 'idden

14

strings. Ha! This's my Elba. Allard thinks
'e's got rid of me, but I live. What can I—
Well for a start I'll make sure Wick an'
Irwin stay on that committee an' through
'em I'll—well I'll concoct something.
Where the 'ell are they?
(*He returns to the window and looks out,
striking a slight pose.*)
From out the snows he loomed, dark,
wraithlike. A hollow menacing voice from
the past.
(*Sounds of footsteps coming up the stairs.*
SCRAWDYKE *turns.* INGHAM, *wearing a
donkey-jacket and baggy jeans, out of
breath, bursts through the door.*)

INGHAM: I'm sorry Mal.
SCRAWDYKE: Where the hell 'ave y' been?
INGHAM: A'm sorry. Oh—uh, uh, A'm sorry, but
well—uh uh, A've just run up 'ere.
SCRAWDYKE: It 'asn't tekken y' two solid hours t' run
up 'ere.
INGHAM: No, no, y're right. But y'see well like,
y'see uh——
SCRAWDYKE: What?
INGHAM: Yes. Well. Y'see—er, something 'appened.
SCRAWDYKE: What?
INGHAM: Well, y'see like, this morning about 'alf
eleven. All t' members o' t' committee
like— Well Allard called us to 'is room
like. Me an' Wick an' Boocock an'——
SCRAWDYKE: I know 'oo t' members o' t' committee
are. I'm its chairman.
INGHAM: Aye, aye, right enough. Well, anyway, 'e
gets us all in there like an' 'e explains like,
well, 'ow 'e's 'ad t' ask you t' leave——
SCRAWDYKE: Ask!

15

INGHAM: —an' 'e sez like 'e's called us in because
we're t' committee of the Sketch Club an'
'ow as 'e 'as t' warn us——

SCRAWDYKE: Warn you?

INGHAM: Aye, well y' know 'ow 'e—A mean, 'e sez
you've been a disruptive influence—A
mean that's 'is phrase—an' 'ow 'e's given
y' chance after chance—A mean A'm not
sayin' 'e's right A'm just tellin' y' what 'e
said.

SCRAWDYKE: Go on.

INGHAM: Yes, well, 'e goes on, t' say 'at 'e doesn't
like t'ave t' do it but 'e'll 'ave t' ask us, as
sort of the representatives of the students
like, not only not t' 'ave anything further t'
do with y' ourselves like, but also t' go
round all t'other students an' tell them as
well. If, 'e sez, any student in future, 'as
anything t' do with y', meets y', talks t' y',
an' 'e finds out like that they 'ave, 'e'll
expel 'em immediately an' tell the
education authorities t' stop their grants
an' 'e'll make sure they don't get in t' any
other art school. 'E sez if 'e doesn't do this
like, an' your—influence isn't stopped—
Well, the 'ole school might 'ave t' close
down.

(SCRAWDYKE *smilingly paces up and down.*)

SCRAWDYKE: I'm not surprised, I'm not surprised. I
could 'ave told y' this would 'appen. I
could 'ave predicted it. 'E's shown 'imself
in 'is true colours. Totalitarian, power mad!

INGHAM: Aye, well that's why A couldn't get up 'ere
on time.

SCRAWDYKE: It didn't tek 'im three hours t' tell y'——

INGHAM: No, no. Well afterwards like, we all, like,

16

'ad a bit of a——

SCRAWDYKE: What did Wick say?

INGHAM: Ah well Wick. Well John—'e said something more or less like you've just said.

SCRAWDYKE: Boocock?

INGHAM: Well 'e seemed t' think like, 'at Allard might just, well 'ave gone just that little bit too far this time, 'e——

SCRAWDYKE: Very radical of 'im. The balanced view. I hate intellectuals! An' what about Elaine Akroyde an' that other emancipated beauty?

INGHAM: Ah well, the two girls, yes——

SCRAWDYKE: What does that mean? "Ah well the two girls yes." What sort of a position is that?

INGHAM: No A di'n't mean that as their——

SCRAWDYKE: Well what did they say?

INGHAM: Well Mal, y' know 'ow they sort of feel——

SCRAWDYKE: That's all they can do, feel. An' what uncompromisin' position did you stoutly defend?

INGHAM: Well, I er—y' know I er, I could er—like, I er, well——

SCRAWDYKE: What did y' say?

INGHAM: Well, A mean um, A can't exactly——

SCRAWDYKE: What did y' decide t' do?

INGHAM: Ah well, Wick, 'e's got a plan.

SCRAWDYKE: What?

INGHAM: Oh well, A think it's better if 'e like, tells y' 'imself when 'e gets 'ere.

SCRAWDYKE: You tell me.

INGHAM: No, no, it'll be better if he——

SCRAWDYKE: You don't agree with it?

INGHAM: Yes, yes, 'course A do. A mean A'm on your side, y' know that.

SCRAWDYKE: Huh!

17

INGHAM: 'E'll tell y' when 'e gets 'ere.

SCRAWDYKE: Well why isn't 'e 'ere now?

INGHAM: Ah well, y' see, that's all part of it.

SCRAWDYKE: Keepin' me 'angin' around up 'ere, freezin', starvin'?

INGHAM: Av'n't y' 'ad owt t' eat?

SCRAWDYKE: 'Ow could A? You were supposed to be bringin' me ten bob.

INGHAM: Oh aye, yes. (*Forks out ten bob note.*)

SCRAWDYKE: Ta. Y' av'n't got a shillin'?

INGHAM: Oh it's out. No.

SCRAWDYKE: Well give us a fag.

INGHAM: Yeh.

SCRAWDYKE: Tipped!

INGHAM: Oh yeh.

SCRAWDYKE: What the 'ell y' smokin' tipped for?

INGHAM: Well y' see A pulled t' wrong thing on a machine.

SCRAWDYKE: Contraceptives. I hate tipped. 'Ow's y' throat?

INGHAM: 't's all right now.

(*Footsteps are heard rapidly coming up stairs.* WICK, *dressed in a lumber jacket and narrow jeans, jumps in grinning.*)

WICK: Aha there 'e is! Public Enemy Number One!

(*Advances into room.*)

Man y've done it this time! 'As Irwin told y'?

SCRAWDYKE: 'E mentioned something.

WICK: Yeh, well, when that little bastard got us in 'is room an' started on the big purge, I nearly burst a blood-vessel man! Mustn't see y', mustn't meet y', mustn't even mention your subversive name in those 'allowed attics. I couldn't believe me ears. I

18

thought for a minute 'e was goin' t' order
us all up t' t' Infirmary for blood tests and
compulsory castration. It's the gas
chambers for anybody 'oo even accidentally
catches sight of a poor photograph of you
mate.

SCRAWDYKE: Y'd better start 'oldin' y' breath then.

WICK: Aar! Y' don't think we're goin' t' tek any
notice do y'? A've never been so incensed!
That little runt tellin' us 'oo we can see!
An' afterwards those two chastity belts on
legs, Akroyde an' Firth, started on about it
all bein' y're own fault. That little
Akroyde's really vicious when she gets
goin'. She nearly clawed me eyes out when
A said we should back you. Didn't she
Irwin?

INGHAM: Aye she nearly touched 'im.

WICK: A'd 'ave touched 'er! I tried t' point out
'at Allard's tramplin' on our basic rights
but there was no arguin' with 'em. An'
Boocock was there in t' middle as usual,
sayin' 'at although Allard's gone too far
you 'ad ignored all 'is warnin's about
skippin' classes, arsin' about, an' all that
crap. An' of course, 'e didn't know what
we ought t' do. Anyway I realized it was
no good so Irwin an' me, we've worked
out a little plan.

SCRAWDYKE: Expatiate.

WICK: Yeh. Look Allard thinks 'e's scared us off
seeing you. 'E thinks we're so scared of
missin' finals an' not gettin' a plastic
diploma we'll obey 'im. At least for a
while, for a few weeks anyway. But even
Allard can't imagine we'll keep away from

19

y' for ever. So all we've got t' do is wait.
For a while we'll 'ave to play it cunnin'.
What we'll do is this. Me and Irwin, we'll
'ave an arrangement with y'. We'll meet y'
on certain nights, at certain pubs on the
outskirts o' town. Y' know, a pub Monday,
another for Tuesday, an' so on like that.
Places where Allard can't possibly 'ave
any spies. Say t' New Inn past Fartown, t'
Clough 'Ouse up Fixby, some pub down
Lockwood, out at Waterloo. We'll all go
there separately an' we'll leave separately.
Me an' Irwin 'ave already started, that's
why we arrived 'ere separately. I ate in t'
Tech canteen an 'e ate at Wrigleys——

INGHAM: Yeh.

WICK: —an' we both came up 'ere by different
routes an' we staggered our arrival.
Anyway in future, if we pass y' on t'
street, we won't even see each other, we'll
cut each other dead. At least, that's what'll
seem to 'appen. But actually we'll 'ave a
secret little sign 'at'll be missed by even
Allard's most observant 'enchlings. An
infinitesimal twitch of the cheek, which'll
mean, we're all t'gether, united, solid. It'll
be so bloody subtle an' we'll be doin' it
right under Allard's nose. 'E'll think 'e's
won when all t' time the'll be this
underground resistance. It'll be great! It'll
be a conspiracy man!
(*Pause.*)
Well what d' y' think?
(SCRAWDYKE *glowers at them, moves, then*
looks at WICK.)

SCRAWDYKE: Phht!

WICK: What's the matter with——?

SCRAWDYKE: Gimme a fag.

INGHAM: Yeh, yeh.

SCRAWDYKE: Not another o' those.

INGHAM: 'S all A've got.

WICK: 'Ere A've got some Woodies.

(SCRAWDYKE *lights fag*.)

SCRAWDYKE: You say that Allard'll think 'e's won. Well if we adopt your bold, darin' proposition, trudgin' miles through snow an' sleet t' remote, freezin' pubs for five minutes furtive mumblin', sneakin' round town twitchin' our cheeks, of course Allard'll think that 'e's won. 'E'll 'ave ev'ry right t' think so. Because 'e will 'ave! It's exactly what 'e wants! I've never 'eard such complete an' supine capitulation masquerading as defiance. Allard did castrate you this mornin'.

WICK: Look A'm just as disgusted by Allard as you are. 'Course we've got t' defy 'im. That's the 'ole bloody idea. But we've got t' play it cunnin'. Meet 'is blunt, naked force with subtlety. It's the only way.

INGHAM: Yeh.

SCRAWDYKE: What 'a you sayin' "Yeh" for?

INGHAM: Well A mean——

SCRAWDYKE: Y' don't mean anything, y' don't think anything an' y' never say anything. Y' never do. 'E's just t' same only 'e expresses it more fluently.

WICK: Aw——

SCRAWDYKE: What a pair you are! Allard insolently treats y' like mentally deficient hens and you boldly strike back by twitchin' y'r cheeks!

21

WICK: I suppose you've got a better idea.

SCRAWDYKE: I have. I always 'ave a better idea. Listen, this's a magnificent opportunity t' do all the things we've alwas talked about. Yesterday evening at 8.25 'e threw me out. With reference to this I 'ave only one regret. That I didn't walk out myself a year ago. Today 'e attempts to stifle your last vestiges of dignity. 'E threatens to expel you if you disobey 'im. Laugh in 'is face like free men an' leave!

WICK: Leave?

INGHAM: But——

SCRAWDYKE: Yes, leave, look the issue's simple. Freedom or serfdom. That's the choice. That's what it is. Surrender to 'im now and your integrity's gone, gone for all time. Whatever y' do in future y'll be utterin' empty noises, standin' on rotten boards. Y'll have betrayed y'selves, sold out, y'll be nothing but self-hatin' eunuchs. You'll know that when the critical moment rose up, you opted for nonentitihood. The choice you must make, an' it can't be shirked, is not just for today or tomorrow but for the rest of your lives. And what 'ave y' t' lose by leavin' now? A one-line question with a one-word answer. Nothing! Finals, N.D.D., what's that? Nothing! Nothing Doing Diploma which'll earn you the glorious privilege of designin' dogfood wrappers or keepin' a roomful of delinquents in order. Where's art in that? Where's life? Where's any form of tangible satisfaction? John. You're the most talented painter 'oo ever walked through those dirty corridors

22

an' attics down in that so-called school of
Art. A man with your potential comes
once in five generations, if that. They
should be down on their knees begging,
begging to help you. They should be
overwhelmed with gratitude that they've
been fortunate enough to earn footnotes in
art history by 'elpin 'Uddersfield's one
chance of puttin' a painter up there in the
top rank alongside Cézanne, Matisse,
Picasso. You are 'Uddersfield's Greatest
Son and Allard treats you like a silly child.
I know painting. I know your work. I say
it is an outrage against the cultural
aspirations of Mankind. You know I don't
say things like this lightly, I don't often
turn my tongue to praise, I don't go
around sprinkling confetti.
An' Irwin, you're a sensitive man, a man
'oo needs bringin' out, nurturin'. A
magnificent draughtsman. The next Dürer.
A man of profound depth. And what do
they do down there? They crush y', whistle
you around like a little dog. And what
about women? Because you 'aven't got the
small talk mentality, because you can't
cavort, make with the easy flippant talk,
they spurn you, snigger behind your back,
don't even see you. They hand us nothing
but contempt. Insults! Insults! Insults! Are
we goin' t' go on takin' it for ever? Flat on
our backs, with their farts in our faces! Is
this the future y' see for y'selves? If it is
then y're not the men I took y' for!

WICK: No! Y're right! We can't let the buggers
keep us down. When I think of all the guff

I've taken from mediocrities! Man I'd like
t' get back at 'em. I'd like t' show——
SCRAWDYKE: Get your own back with a vengeance!
WICK: Yeh.
INGHAM: Yeh, well, the's a lot in what y'—but, like,
if we did, like, leave, A mean, y' say the's
nothing down there, N.D.D. But what like
could we do? An' then there's questions
such as, well, like money, A mean . . .
SCRAWDYKE: You're revellin' in theory, Irwin. Let's
consider now the present concrete situation.
Allard 'as issued a challenge. We must
accept that challenge or resign all claim to
being men. I face the challenge, I issue a
retort. Don't go back to the Art School.
Give it the two fingers. Let's form ourselves
into a political party. We'll never 'ave a
better opportunity and just think of the
date. January the First. Man it's designed
for such destinial action!
WICK: Haha, yeh. Ey yeh, January 1st!
INGHAM: But——
SCRAWDYKE: Our first goal will be to smash Allard. Our
ultimate goal'll be t' realize all our dreams,
take our proper place in the scheme of
things, an' achieve absolute power!
WICK: Well it's an idea. Yeh! If we——
SCRAWDYKE: "If we". What d'you mean, "if we"? What
'ave we got t' lose? You agree there's no
future bein' a cog in Allard's wheel.
WICK: Yeh.
SCRAWDYKE: So what do we lose?
WICK: Nothing.
SCRAWDYKE: Walk out. Think of the look on 'is face.
WICK: Haha. Yeh.
SCRAWDYKE: We've got the imagination and the will.

24

WICK: Yeh. Come on let's do it! Let's make something 'appen. I'm sick of toein' the line, day in day out, in this provincial ghetto. We'll tell 'im where 'e gets off! What d'y' say, Irwin?

INGHAM: Oh but A mean . . . a Party.

SCRAWDYKE: Well?

INGHAM: But A mean, a Party. The's only three of us.

SCRAWDYKE: 'Itler started with seven.

WICK: An' Marx started with one, 'imself.

SCRAWDYKE: Exactly.

INGHAM: But A mean, what could we do? A mean in 'Uddersfield?

SCRAWDYKE: Just the place. The most unexpected quarter is just the place to launch a surprise offensive. Ev'ry strategist knows that.

INGHAM: An offensive? On what?

SCRAWDYKE: The minds. The minds of the nation.

WICK: We'll make this our 'eadquarters.

SCRAWDYKE: Members'll come rollin' in.

INGHAM: Oh but A mean . . . we 'aven't even got enough chairs.

SCRAWDYKE: You're deceived by appearances, Irwin. You think because all you can see is three blokes in a drab room that's all there is. I see the reality; We are the germ. The revolution isn't in this room. It's up 'ere. Willpower. The first and last necessity. With it y' can do anythin', without it nothin'. An' we've got it.

WICK: Because we're small now means nothing. A virus can kill—what?—an elephant.

INGHAM: But A mean 'oo's goin' t'—'oo's goin' t' tek any—'oo's goin' to join?

SCRAWDYKE: Ultimately ev'rybody, whether they like it

or not.

WICK: Haha.

SCRAWDYKE: . . . t' begin with kindred spirits. All over the country, on ev'ry street corner, the young an' frustrated are waitin'. They feel a deep resentment, a pent up force. They don't know 'ow t' use it. They're tired of the old slogans. They yearn, they aspire, they wait for leaders. We are those leaders. We're here! They'll soon find out.

WICK: Aye. And we shall——

SCRAWDYKE: Of course we've got to start off with a concrete plan. We've got t' nobble Allard and do it in such a way that it's a symbolic gesture.

WICK: Yeh what could we do?

SCRAWDYKE: One decisive act. Don't theorize, do!

WICK: What can we—it's got t' be——

SCRAWDYKE: Well are you with us?

WICK: Are you goin' t' 'elp us get Allard?

INGHAM: Well——

SCRAWDYKE: Are y' goin' to join us on the road to power?

INGHAM: Well er——

SCRAWDYKE: D' y' want it?

INGHAM: What?

SCRAWDYKE: Power.

INGHAM: Er—er—er—uh—well—A wouldn't mind.

WICK: Great! Three 'oo made a revolution!

SCRAWDYKE: Two an' a third. Now we've got to find— we've got t' get Allard an' at the same time—a symbol. We've got t' astonish the world.

WICK: Switch on a spotlight that'll illuminate——

SCRAWDYKE: Of course the best thing'd be——

WICK: What?

SCRAWDYKE: . . . to kill 'im!

WICK: Assassination!

INGHAM: Oh Mal, A mean——

SCRAWDYKE: It's beautiful, it's simple, it's direct, an' above all it's violent.

WICK: Clean an' decisive.

SCRAWDYKE: But it could create sympathy for 'im.

WICK: We've got to avoid that.

INGHAM: Aye, and we'd get sentenced to——

SCRAWDYKE: There's something t' be said for the short jail sentence.

WICK: Yeh, well A suppose it could make an impact.

SCRAWDYKE: Yeh, quick martyrdom, couple o' weeks inside, then y're out t' pick up the sympathy.

WICK: An' we needn't go in.

SCRAWDYKE: 'Course not. We could let a comparatively inessential member take the rap. Whilst we, the real brains, exploit it outside. Irwin could go in.

INGHAM: Oh come off it Mal.

WICK: What's the matter? Y'd be a martyr man! Y'd get all the glamour. Think of all the sympathetic birds comin' t' see y' on visitin' days.

INGHAM: Oh——

SCRAWDYKE: 'Course y' wouldn't actually be able t' touch 'em.

WICK: But think of all t' voluptuous dreams y' could 'ave in y' cell. The party in its munificence'd provide y' with a jockstrap free of charge. What an offer! The Movement's First Martyr. Y'd rank wi' Joan of Arc man!

INGHAM: Not in a jockstrap A wouldn't.

27

(*They all laugh.*)

WICK: Congratulations, Irwin. Sometimes——

SCRAWDYKE: Yeh.

(WICK *gets out fags, hands them around.*)

So we rule out assassination.

WICK: What about kidnappin' 'im?

SCRAWDYKE: No, we've got t' show 'im up. Make 'im reveal 'imself for what 'e is. 'Ow?—'Ow could we——

WICK: Make 'im resign.

SCRAWDYKE: —got to—first of all we've got t' get 'im. I know! We'll kidnap 'im.

WICK: Great! Then do what?

SCRAWDYKE: Er— Got it!

WICK: }
INGHAM: } What?

SCRAWDYKE: Blackmail!

WICK: Blackmail?

INGHAM: What wi'?

SCRAWDYKE: What with! What with! Y've bin down in that art school four years an' y' don't know what with?

INGHAM: Well A mean like—'e might be a bit unfair like but——

SCRAWDYKE: Y're blind Irwin! I saw it immediately. Margaret Thwaite!

WICK: Margaret Thwaite?

SCRAWDYKE: Margaret Thwaite.

WICK: Margaret Thwaite!

INGHAM: Margaret Thwaite?

SCRAWDYKE: Allard knocked 'er off!

INGHAM: Oh well A mean, 'e might 'ave necked with 'er a bit like at Chris'mas parties but——

SCRAWDYKE: 'E did more than that.

INGHAM: What?

SCRAWDYKE: 'E 'ad 'er in 'is car.

28

INGHAM: We've only 'er word for it.

SCRAWDYKE: We've more than that. I've seen with me own eyes——

WICK: I've seen 'er in that bloody car with 'im.

INGHAM: Well I've seen 'er in 'is——

WICK: Then 'ow can y' say we've only 'er word then?

INGHAM: Well in 'is car, A mean what's that? Just a lift like, A mean we didn't actually see 'im, well y' know . . .

SCRAWDYKE: She told me about it. I know the inside story. I make it my bizness t' ferret out these things. I'm not seduced by surface appearances. I never ignore the slightest scrap of seemingly irrelevant data. I keep my eyes skinned, I gather, I co-relate, I wait, an' then when I'm ready, I pounce! Allard knows that I know what there is t' be known. But 'e's 'ad t' move cannily . . . bide 'is time an' wait. To 'ave slung me out years ago would 'ave been too dangerous. I might 'ave spewed out the lot. So 'e's waited an' waited till the 'ole thing's receded into the past. I've been a marked man in that school for two years. Allard wears the mask of the artist, the guardian of sensibility, the up'older of good taste. 'E's considered fit t' guard an' guide young minds. But we all know that this mask is nothing but—a mask! Be'ind it cringes the real Allard, 'oo's int'rested in one thing an' one thing only——

WICK: 'Is career.

SCRAWDYKE: Power! We must strip the mask from the face of depravity. We must tear it away! Rip it! Smash it! Obliterate it! So that the

29

world may stamp with both its feet on the insect beneath.

WICK: What are we goin' t' blackmail 'im in t' doing?

SCRAWDYKE: First things first. We've got t' let Allard know y've walked out.

WICK: Yeh. Well what's the best way?

SCRAWDYKE: Go and tell 'im.

INGHAM: Oh—can't we just like—send 'im a little note?

WICK: Yeh. Maybe Irwin's got summat there.

SCRAWDYKE: That's not leavin' it's sneakin' out. I didn't send any notes.

INGHAM: Oh no, but like, 'e threw you out.

SCRAWDYKE: That's what I let 'im think. I'd been waitin' for the right opportunity. If I'd just walked out any old time I'd 'ave put 'im on 'is guard.

WICK: Ey, y' mean y' planned for 'im t'——?

SCRAWDYKE: I'm not sayin' I planned for it t' 'appen yesterday. That wouldn't be honest and A don't want to mislead y'. But y' know all the little things I've kept doin' t' niggle 'im. Well they weren't accidents. They seemed like accidents becos that's the way I wanted it. I knew 'at one time or another 'e'd catch me in some little infraction an' it'd incite 'im t' boot me out. That wasn't just an ordinary smoke I 'ad yesterday. It seemed like an ordinary smoke t' the unobservant eye but far from it. That smoke was worked out t' the last detail. Why d' y' think I went right into the corridor? Why d' y' think I went right up outside 'is door? If I'd just been after an illicit drag I could 'ave 'ad it in class be'ind

30

that plaster cast.

WICK: Aye y' could.

INGHAM: I thought y' went out there becos y' thought Allard was over t' road in pottery, an' like, y' din't want t' leave smoke in t' room. A mean that's just what A thought——

SCRAWDYKE: That's what you were intended t' think. I knew 'e was in 'is room, I've got a sixth sense for that man's movements. I didn't know whether 'e'd fall for it there and then, 'e might not see me or 'e might just warn me. But I knew 'at when 'e did fall for my little trap 'e'd follow it with all this purge stuff an' the scene'd be set for this. Was I surprised when y' told me?

INGHAM: Well—no—y' didn't seem——

SCRAWDYKE: There you are. You'll take an ultimatum down telling 'im y've left.

INGHAM: An ultimatum!

SCRAWDYKE: I'll write it for y'!

WICK: Eh, what are we goin' t' call this party?

SCRAWDYKE: Oh now, let's see—uh—it wants t' be—the party of—dynamic yes—I've got it—the Party of Dynamic Erection!

WICK: Just the name!

SCRAWDYKE: We're against the Eunarchy. We're against the castrated wherever they are. We're against all those 'oo want to reduce us to their level.

WICK: Yeh. And when are we goin' t' stage the putsch?

SCRAWDYKE: Now let's see—what is it today? Thursday, Friday tomorra. Give ourselves a week. We'll do it a week tomorra. We'll do it on Friday, January 9th.

31

WICK: Great! That will be the day! The Day of
Dynamic Erection!

SCRAWDYKE: The Day. The Day of Decision. The Day
of Retribution. The Day of Will.

WICK: The Day of Wrath. The Day of Truth.

SCRAWDYKE: The Day of the New Fist.

WICK: The First Day.

SCRAWDYKE: The Last Day.

WICK: The Birth Day.

SCRAWDYKE: The Death Day.

WICK: The Day of Iron.

SCRAWDYKE: The Day of Steel.

WICK: The Day of Aluminium.

SCRAWDYKE: The Day of Molybdenum.

WICK: The Day of Lead.

SCRAWDYKE: The Day of Plastic.

WICK: The Day of Mud.

SCRAWDYKE: The Day of Porridge.

WICK: The Day of Wet Cardboard.

SCRAWDYKE: The Day of Horsehair Underpants.

WICK: The Day of Chewed Grass Wigs.
(*They jump about with glee. They let out
high-pitched yelps like dogs.*)

BLACKOUT

END OF SCENE 1

32

SCENE 2

SCRAWDYKE *bursts in. Switches on light. It is dark outside.*
He bats snow off himself.

SCRAWDYKE: Oooough! Sssss. Faah! No shillin'! Oh no
'eat, no food, 'aven't eaten. Not even any
comfort t'——
Oh, what a feeble— There it was all laid
out an' I didn't, I couldn't. Invites me
down 'ome after—it's warm, it's cosy,
nobody about, gives me coffee. She lays
back on the sofa. I couldn't even relax
enough t' tek me coat off. Stutterin',
mumblin'. "Well I er used t' drink more
tea like, y' know, than er I, er I, y' know
like drink um coffee now. A mean A've no
real preference—" Wallpaper. Size of 'er
kitchen. Is it still snowin'? Anything but
what I really wanted. The way she sat on
that sofa—the way 'er eyes. Aargh, they
mock me. So they should. What a spineless!
"Come an' sit down Malcolm." Oh stop it
A can't stand it. I perch there like a rigid
board on t' end, she moves slightly towards
me and what did I do? Jumped up! She
wanted it, I know. An' I— What is this
block? What is it? Why am I so in'ibited?
Why? Why me? All I want is t' be treat
like a 'uman being!
She told me about Irwin cowerin' outside

33

Allard's office. Allard comes out, Irwin just
vaguely shoves t' ultimatum at 'im an'
scuttles away. She saw it. Wait until I—
Oh I talk about 'im. What about me!
I've 'ad it now. She'll never look at me
again. That's down the—what am I goin'
to do? What am I goin' t' do? What!
I've got t' see 'er again!
Oh I can't 'ow could I—
Fix up a date! Phone 'er.
I'd never dare. I've never been able t' do
things like that.
Write?
Oh she might show it 'er pals. They'd all
giggle.
No she wouldn't, she's not like that.
After t'night she'll 'ave nothing but
contempt.
No she'll think y' were just shy. Could be
in y're favour. Reserved. Not too fast.
But even if she does, 'ow can I see 'er?
An accident. Make it seem like an accident.
She'd see through it.
No she wouldn't. Not if y' worked it
properly.
But 'ow?
Go to her place.
I couldn't. 'Ow'd that seem like an
accident.
Say y' were just passin'. Say you'd been t'
see Mick Norris. 'E lives down that way.
But what if 'er mother's in?
She won't be. She works nights. Y' know
that.
But I'd never dare knock. What'd I say?
You were just passin'.

34

I'd never get it out.

Repeat it over an' over again till it comes
out automatic. Chant it to y'self on y' way
down there.

But even if A could. What when A get in?
The Party man. The bloody Party. That'll
boost you in 'er eyes.

An' then what?

Well get 'er in the mood. Then, then—just
throw y'self in.

Oh it's impossible.

It's not.

It is.

It isn't.

It is.

You can.

I can't.

You can.

I can't.

You can.

I can't.

You can! Don't brood about after. Just get
in. Get in. That by itself 'll show 'er
something. Even if y' don't get started this
time y'll be keepin' the ball rollin'.

Well I—

What else is the' t' do?

Nothing.

Well do it!

When?

Tomorra night.

Not tomorra night. I need time.

It's got t' be. Y've got t' get in quick
before it's too late.

Oh—

Y' c'n see that can't you?

35

I—
You can see it can't you?
I suppose so—
Good!
What time?
She catches the nine o'clock trolley. Be
down at 'er place at—ten.
'S too early. She'd suspect.
No, no, she won't know 'ow long y've been
at Mick's— So y'll do it?
Yes. I'll try.
Not try. Do! .
I'll do it. Yes. I'll do it. I'll— The Party.
Yes, that'll astound 'er. Oh if I can bring
this off, fuck the Party. Ann'd be my real
conquest; not all this Dynamic Nonsense.
Well I've got some action. Got people
around me. That's something. I hate bein'
all on me— All those years I lived out in
Bailiff Bridge, seven miles away, out on the
edge, ev'ry week-end pinin' away in silence.
'Uddersfield's always been the centre t' me.
Came in ev'ry day t' conquer it. Along the
spoke into the hub. An' all this time I've
never felt—I still don't belong. Not my
town. I'll make it my town! I'll make it sit
up! I'll make the bloody world think I am
'Uddersfield. Inseparably linked,
Scrawdyke, ah, yes, 'Uddersfield. Leavin'
'ome that was a good move. I'll get Wick
and Irwin to move in 'ere. Then I won't be
on me own. I'll get Ann. That'd be the
biggest— Yes, I must act an' I must act
now!
Ooo 't's so cold! Get t' bed!
(*During the following he removes coat, puts*

it on bed, removes shoes.)
Got t' try an' sleep. If I could only sleep
t'night. Blank mind. Secret of success 's a
blank mind. Yes. Just lay there. Switch
off— Ooo it's bloody cold! Well never—
(*Switches light off.* BLACKOUT. *Gets into
bed.*)
Friday, January 2nd now. This 's got t' be
the year. Yes. Now come on relax, go
blank. Then—the 'ole thing's—only a
question of doin' it.

SCENE 3

Lights up. Grey noonday light. SCRAWDYKE *is sitting up in bed.* DENNIS NIPPLE, *a tallish slouching lumbering man of twenty-six, in shabby duffle-coat, with the hood up, is standing.*

NIPPLE: Noe, no y' wrong.

SCRAWDYKE: I'm tellin' t' it was green!

NIPPLE: Noe it wasn't it was blue.

SCRAWDYKE: It was green.

NIPPLE: Noe blue.

SCRAWDYKE: I should know, it was my jacket.

NIPPLE: Well Ai saw it.

SCRAWDYKE: You saw it! I wore it. For two years.

NIPPLE: Noe not for so long.

SCRAWDYKE: 'Ow the 'ell d' you know?

NIPPLE: Ai c'n remember.

SCRAWDYKE: Y' timed it?

NIPPLE: Noe, but A know it wasn't so long.

SCRAWDYKE: You can't even remember the colour of it.

NIPPLE: Ai can. It was a sort of dingy blue.

SCRAWDYKE: It was a mellow green.

NIPPLE: Noe y' can't call it green. Y' might say it 'ad a very slight greenish tinge, but it was blue.

SCRAWDYKE: You obviously can't tell the diff'rence between blue an' green.

NIPPLE: Noe it's you 'oo caan't tell the diff'rence. Y' call y'self an artist an' y' can't——

SCRAWDYKE: I know that jacket. You're colour blind.

Y've got a very poor visual sense. Words are your medium.

NIPPLE: That may be. But A'm sensitive t' colour an' shade. Ai caan't paint but Ai c'n see.

SCRAWDYKE: Then why d' y' wear them thick specs?

NIPPLE: They don't stop colours comin' through. They intensify.

SCRAWDYKE: They blur and distort.

NIPPLE: Noe, you're just makin' excuses for y're own lack of observation.

SCRAWDYKE: Look, when a man wears a jacket for two blasted years 'e ought t' know what colour it is.

NIPPLE: Noe, yoo mustn't ever 'ave looked at it. Ai suppose, y' were too deep in intellectual thought as usual. Yoo don't notice what goes on around y'. Ai do. Ai've got a keen perception for the world of the senses. Sights, sounds, odours, tactile titillations. I'm a walking seismograph of sensual innuendo. A feast on 'em. They're the raw stuff from which Ai weave.

SCRAWDYKE: Balls! Y' can't see six inches in front of y' face. Y' couldn't smell a roomful of dead elephants. If a time-bomb went off in y're pocket— Oh I'm not goin' t' argue with y'. This nonsense about the jacket shows 'ow perceptive you are.

NIPPLE: Now y' just tryin' t'— It's yoo 'o's unperceptive. Only yoo could even imagine it was green.

SCRAWDYKE: Listen mate. I'll tell y' 'ow unperceptive you are. If that jacket 'ad a tendency towards any other colour than green, it was brown.

NIPPLE: Oh noe. Ai admit it wasn't pure blue.

There was an 'int of green, just an 'int. But
A don't know where y' get brown from.

SCRAWDYKE: An 'int of green. It was green! Green with
a tendency towards brown.

NIPPLE: Ai never saw any brown.

SCRAWDYKE: You wouldn't. You only see what y' want
to.

NIPPLE: Ai saw it as blooey green.

SCRAWDYKE: Listen that sort of corderoy jacket mellows
with wear, with the weather on it, an' the
green takes on a——

NIPPLE: It wasn't corderoy.

SCRAWDYKE: Of course it was corderoy.

NIPPLE: Nah, nah, it were a sort of stuff made up t'
look like corderoy.

SCRAWDYKE: It was the real thing. 'Ow the 'ell would
you know?

NIPPLE: Noe real corderoy's not like that. Y' c'n
tell if y' see real corderoy. Y' c'n tell, it's a
subtle diff'rence. It 'as a richer sort o'
texture.

SCRAWDYKE: It was bought as corderoy. I should know.

NIPPLE: Hee, hee, y' were taken in.

SCRAWDYKE: I was not taken in. I know corderoy. I
asked for a corderoy jacket an' that's what
I got.

NIPPLE: Noe yoo can't afford reel corderoy.

SCRAWDYKE: It 'ad the bloody label in it.

NIPPLE: Oh well Ai suppose they called it corderoy.
A mean that's 'ow they sell it t' people like
you. But Ai——

SCRAWDYKE: So you can discern that a jacket isn't
corderoy, even if it looks like corderoy,
feels like corderoy, an' is called corderoy.
You 'ave a mystical sixth sense for the real
corderoy.

40

NIPPLE: Noe but Ai c'n tell. Yoo're not clo'es conscious like me.

SCRAWDYKE: I know clothes. I don't dress by accident. I choose my outfit with care. I reject fashionable elegance. I present an image, haggard, gaunt, unkempt. I dress with style.

NIPPLE: Hee hee after the Revolution ev'rybody 'll 'ave t' dress like yoo. It'll be the 'ight of fashion. Hee hee. An' mai books'll be made compulsory readin'.

SCRAWDYKE: You'll allow your work to be published? A thought that was beneath your dignity?

NIPPLE: Noe, noe, Ai never said that. Ai said 'at public honours 'old no temptation for mee. The reel writer, the great writer dismisses prizes an' honours as unworthy of 'im. The only tribute 'e accepts is the readin' of 'is work. 'E stands alone, remote. A great crag risin' out of the plain of ordinariness.

SCRAWDYKE: Where the 'ell's Irwin with those chips A sent 'im for?

NIPPLE: Where's 'e gone for 'em?

SCRAWDYKE: That place up there, just opposite.

NIPPLE: South Parade.

SCRAWDYKE: No that street just opposite. Y' c'n see it through t' winder.

NIPPLE: That's South Parade.

(NIPPLE *moves to window, looks out.*)

SCRAWDYKE: It's not.

NIPPLE: It is. They've put cinders down on Chapel 'Ill.

SCRAWDYKE: I know that.

NIPPLE: All is crowned in white. T' roofs o' those shops opposite. Even t' Public Bog over there is mantled with flaky ermine. That

41

letter box at t' bottom of South Parade———

SCRAWDYKE: It's not called South Parade.

NIPPLE: It is.

SCRAWDYKE: Oh well A'm not goin' t' argue with y'. Y're disputatous. I 'av'n't 'ad owt to eat for forty-three hours.

NIPPLE: Once Ai went for longer 'an that without food.

SCRAWDYKE: When?

NIPPLE: Last summer after that party at Barry Lawton's when me mother locked me out by mistake. Ai decided t' see 'ow long A could go without food an' sleep. Ai decided t' seek the unknown vistas of the 'allucinated mind. Ai embarked on a pilgrimage to the dream city of surreal experience. Ai wanted t' see if Ai could induce 'allucinations.

SCRAWDYKE: Your 'ole life's an 'allucination.

NIPPLE: Noe, noe, let me tell y'.

SCRAWDYKE: I wouldn't dream of stoppin' y'.

NIPPLE: Ai came into town an' as Ai walked about Ai fell into a trance. Ev'rything Ai encountered took on a new shape, a new form, a new meanin'—Ai seemed t' float through the streets. The crowds loomed past me like crazy phantoms. The girls in their summer frocks were like diaphanous chatterin' birds ready t' take wing an' soar through the air. The trolley-buses floated, suspended, great red toys glidin' nowhere, 'ither and thither, to an' fro— Their 'uman cargoes no more than playthings. The 'ole scene no more than a surreal kaleidoscope pageant of insubstantial seemin'. Hee, hee— Then Ai went down

Leeds Road t' the Gas Works, just t' look at it, just t' experience it. Ai stood there an' it rohze before me. Shimmerin'— Pulsatin'— Its chimneys became dark minarets against the 'azy blue canopy of the 'eavens. Its gasometers were—were 'eavin' symbols of dark leashed power. Its coolin' towers were soarin' mirage palaces, leapin' t' block out the life-givin' light. An' the 'ole mesmeric vision belched an' fumed its noxious vapours. A cathedral dedicated to evil. The very ground trembled. Ai felt asphyxiated. The spittle dried in mai throat. Ai choked an' gasped in vain. The terrible, ghastly, impingin' vision clawed at me tryin' t' drag me in. With overwhelmin' force it sucked at me. Suckin' me t' destruction! With a last utter, final frenzy Ai managed to turn—an' stagger away. (*Pause.*)

SCRAWDYKE: It's a terrible place, that Gasworks. T' Coʋncil should be told about it.
(NIPPLE, *still entranced, doesn't reply.*)
If that's what it does to innocent young mystics they ought to put a screen round it.

NIPPLE: Hee hee.
(WICK *and* INGHAM *come in.* INGHAM *is carrying* SCRAWDYKE'S *chips. They both raise their arms and give the salute—*INGHAM *also raises the chips.*)

WICK:
INGHAM: } Hail Scrawdyke!
(SCRAWDYKE *salutes from bed.*)

SCRAWDYKE: Hail Scrawdyke! Where did y' go for these chips—Heckmondwyke?

INGHAM: No. A went up South Parade.

43

NIPPLE: Hee hee.

WICK: Aha Nipple. The Greatest Sucker of 'em all. . . .

(SCRAWDYKE *gets up and puts his jacket, coat and shoes on.*)

NIPPLE: Oh don't start crackin' all those corney——

WICK: So y' don't like my gags?

NIPPLE: They're in bad taste.

WICK: What could be in better taste than a Nipple?

(*Makes a sucking shape with his lips.*)

NIPPLE: Waah, that's not funny.

SCRAWDYKE: Get on wi' that banner.

(INGHAM *starts working.*)

WICK: Sorry A'm late Mal.

NIPPLE: Ai suppose that was the party salute?

WICK: Ey! Does 'e——?

SCRAWDYKE: I've appointed 'im the Party Archivist an' Minister of Records. We need an 'istorian on the spot from the word go.

WICK: Oh yeh.

NIPPLE: That's not a proper salute.

WICK: It's a perfectly good salute.

NIPPLE: Noe, no, y' shouldn't bend y'r arm like that. Y' should raise it like this.

WICK: You're findin' a lot of fault, Nipple. It's an honour t' be invited t' join this Party, especially at this early stage.

NIPPLE: Ai don't see——

SCRAWDYKE: Look, either you accept my authority, an authority unanimously vested in me, or y' c'n push off.

NIPPLE: Waaarh.

WICK: Well?

(NIPPLE *shuffles.*)

NIPPLE: —awright.

44

WICK: All right what?

NIPPLE: All right Ai agree.

WICK: Raise y' right arm like this.
(NIPPLE *does*.)
Do this with y' fingers.

NIPPLE: Waagh, it makes it look as though y'
tryin' t' grasp something.

WICK: We are tryin' t' grasp something y' silly
bastard. Now repeat after me. I Dennis
Nipple.

NIPPLE: That's not mai name.

WICK: Then what is y're name?

NIPPLE: Dennis Charles Nipple.

WICK: O.K., I Dennis Charles Nipple.

NIPPLE: Ai Dennis Charles Nipple.

WICK: On this 2nd day of January.

NIPPLE: Is that the right date?

WICK: Of course it is!

NIPPLE: Wait a minute it's not. It's the Third t'day.

SCRAWDYKE: It's the bloody second. Get on with it!

WICK: On this second day of January.

NIPPLE: Oh well, it's your mistake. On this 2nd day
of January.

WICK: Swear an oath of personal allegiance to my
Leader Malcolm Scrawdyke.

NIPPLE: Swear an oath of personal allegiance to the
Leader Malcolm Scrawdyke.

WICK: And through absolute obedience to his will
to the aims and struggle of the Dynamic
Erectionist Party.

NIPPLE: And through absolute obedience to 'is will
to the aims an' struggles of the Dynamic
Erectionist Party.
(SCRAWDYKE *has finished his chips. He puts
on a record of Tommy Ladnier*.)

SCRAWDYKE: I've been thinkin'. We need a new calendar.

This is the New Year One, an' we need
new names for the months.

WICK: Yeh, that's a great idea man.

SCRAWDYKE: All the old names are after Roman Gods.
We're openin' up a new Pantheon.

WICK: We'll give 'em our names.

SCRAWDYKE: Exactly. January, the first month, becomes
the month of Scrawdyke, February becomes
Blagden, March, Ingham, an' April Nipple.

WICK: Oho, Nipple. We can't call a month Nipple.
Y'll have t' change y' name.

NIPPLE: Ai'm not changin' mai name.

WICK: All y' need's a pseudonym—Papworthy,
Titteringham.

NIPPLE: Noe.

WICK: Dennis Erotogenic-hyphen-Zone.

NIPPLE: Ai'm not ashamed of mai name.

SCRAWDYKE: It'll soon lose its 'umorous connotations
when we come to power.

WICK: Anybody found smilin' durin' the month of
Nipple will be arrested immediately on a
charge of insolence. The next eight lucky
beggars 'oo join this party get a month
named after 'em. What other movement
can offer a similar incentive?

SCRAWDYKE: I've thought of another thing. We must
'ave a magazine. An official organ.

WICK: With a name like Dynamic Erection we
can't do without it. What about callin' it
Hard Facts.

SCRAWDYKE: Yeh. No I've thought of a name—the
Muckshifter.

WICK: Just the job.

NIPPLE: No, y' don't want a name like that. It's too
mundane. Y' want something with an aura,
something upliftin' spiritual.

46

SCRAWDYKE: That's its name and you're its editor.

NIPPLE: Waah.

SCRAWDYKE: Now let's get on with plannin' the putsch.

WICK: Right. Now next Friday, Scrawdyke the Ninth, we're goin' to whip a paintin' from t' Art Gallery. We're goin' t' bring it 'ere, right? Then later in t' evenin' we're goin' t' kidnap Allard an' blackmail 'im int' smashin' t' paintin'. We're goin' t' say smash it or we'll spill the beans about Margaret Thwaite. 'E'll smash it and then we'll shout it to the world!

SCRAWDYKE: An' that my friends will be our lever to everlastin' fame. Now t' first part, t' first phase of the operation 'll be the raid on t' Art Gallery.

(SCRAWDYKE *goes and switches the record off*.)

Now let's work this out. Come on Irwin. Right so we arrive at the entrance. Come on Irwin!

(*They start to act it out*.)

WICK: Right. So we're in the entrance 'all.

SCRAWDYKE: We look around.

WICK: The's an old bird comin' out o' t' library.

NIPPLE: The's somebody comin' down t' stairs.

SCRAWDYKE: Ignore 'em. Walk casually t' the lift.

WICK: 'O's got t' portfolio?

SCRAWDYKE: Irwin.

(*He gets it*.)

INGHAM: Oh ta.

NIPPLE: The lift's got somebody in it.

SCRAWDYKE: No it 'asn't.

NIPPLE: It 'as!

SCRAWDYKE: No it 'asn't! It's never used at this time.

WICK: Well if it 'as we walk up.

47

SCRAWDYKE: Emergency plan.

WICK: Aye. We get in the lift.

(*They squeeze together in a tight square.*)

SCRAWDYKE: Come on. Now I'm nearest the button.

NIPPLE: No Ai'm nearest the button.

SCRAWDYKE: Which side is it?

INGHAM: Er—that side.

SCRAWDYKE: Then move over.

NIPPLE: Ai don't see——

SCRAWDYKE: I press the button.

NIPPLE: Oh.

SCRAWDYKE: Right. We're on our way up.

WICK: Zzzzzzzzzzzzzzzzzzzzzzz——

NIPPLE: Why——

SCRAWDYKE: Shh! No talkin'! We're there.

WICK: Open t' gates.

SCRAWDYKE: Out.

WICK: Come on Irwin!

INGHAM: Oh aye yeh.

SCRAWDYKE: Quick look round.

WICK: An' we go through the turnstile.

SCRAWDYKE: Good we're in. T' modern stuff's in this first gallery.

WICK: There's somebody down t' far end!

NIPPLE: Ai don't see anybody.

SCRAWDYKE: That's becos y're 'alf blind. Disperse, look casual, go on Irwin look at that—look at that Sutherland.

INGHAM: Er—where is it?

WICK: Down there by t' sink.

INGHAM: Oh.

WICK: I'll go up near t' entrance.

(NIPPLE *looks at* SCRAWDYKE's *self-portrait.*)

NIPPLE: Hee hee. Ai'll look at this thing.

SCRAWDYKE: Don't be funny. Get down there. Just up from Irwin. An' be casual.

NIPPLE: Waah.

SCRAWDYKE: An' I'll look at this wall.

(*Pause.*)

WICK: They've gone!

SCRAWDYKE: Action stations! Wick cover t' entrance.
Nipple you watch t' exit at t' other end.
Go on, get a move on. Irwin you come t'
me wi' t' portfolio. We go t' t' Spencer,
which is on this wall.

NIPPLE: No it's not there.

SCRAWDYKE: 'Course it is. That's where it 'angs, on this
wall.

NIPPLE: Noe it's down 'ere on this wall.

WICK: Wait a minute Mal 'e may be right.

SCRAWDYKE: I know where it is.

NIPPLE: It's over there.

WICK: A'm not sure but A think it's down 'ere.

SCRAWDYKE: No.

WICK: Irwin.

INGHAM: Well er like, A'm not sure, A'm not sayin'
'at anybody's really er—y' know, like—A
mean A don't want t' be dogmatic——

SCRAWDYKE: Come on man! Ev'ry second counts!

INGHAM: Well t' t' best of me er—A seem t'
remember like, 'at it's on that wall where
you are Mal.

SCRAWDYKE: Where?

INGHAM: Er—a bit further up like, no, no, up that
way.

SCRAWDYKE: Right. Come on. Keep watch. O.K.
I-lift-it-off-its-'ooks-an' slowly, slowly,
gently bring-it-down. 'Old the bag open.
Ease it in. Got it.

(INGHAM *drops portfolio*.)

Don't let it go!

INGHAM: Oh—sorry.

49

WICK: We look around. T' attendant's comin'.

SCRAWDYKE: He isn't. Irwin get in t' lift wi' t' paintin'. Wick you with 'im.

WICK: Fine.

SCRAWDYKE: Nipple, you an' me'll saunter casually down t' stairs. We all meet at t' bottom.

WICK: Right. Zzzzzzzzzzzzzzz——

SCRAWDYKE: Right off we go.

(*They walk side by side, round and round, the other two.*)

NIPPLE: That's not saunterin'.

SCRAWDYKE: 'Course it is.

NIPPLE: Noe it's not. Yoo don't know 'ow t' saunter. This's a saunter.

SCRAWDYKE: I saunter in my own way.

NIPPLE: Nobody'd guess. Noe this's a saunter.

SCRAWDYKE: THAT 'eavy, clumpin' torpor.

NIPPLE: Well it's better'n what yoo're doin'. Y' like a jerkin' spastic.

SCRAWDYKE: Ask anybody what I'm doin' an' they'd tell y' I'm saunterin'. Ask 'em what you're doin' an' they'd be 'ard pressed t' tell y' were movin'.

WICK: —zzzzzzz!

NIPPLE: The's nothin' wrong with the way Ai walk.

SCRAWDYKE: 'Ow would you know, y've never done any.

NIPPLE: Aar, yoo 'ave no grace in y' movements.

SCRAWDYKE: Of course I 'ave. I know 'ow t' saunter.

NIPPLE: Noe.

SCRAWDYKE: This's the essence of saunterin'.

NIPPLE: Noe, noe, that's not saunterin'.

WICK: Ey, 'ow long is it goin' to tek you two t' saunter down 'ere? We've bin 'ere ten minutes. Shall we go up an' down again t' give y' time?

SCRAWDYKE: No we're there.

50

WICK: Right. Out we get.

INGHAM: Ee A've got cramp standin' still like that.

WICK: The's a point there Mal, we sh'll get down 'ere before you. We can't 'ang around.

SCRAWDYKE: Exactly, I've foreseen that.

NIPPLE: Then why did y' 'ave 'em goin' down before us then?

SCRAWDYKE: As soon as y' get t' t' bottom get out. Irwin goes out immediately wi' t' portfolio. You say "Good-bye" to 'im, "See y' tomorra." 'E goes out. You make sure nobody follers 'im, then just stroll out.

WICK: Can't I saunter?

SCRAWDYKE: If y' know 'ow. Irwin you walk down t' steps, fairly quickly, but don't run, just a nice brisk walk, an' make y' way 'ere. Now Wick you foller 'im out, y' can watch 'im safely across Ramsden Street out o' t' corner of y're eye.

WICK: Yeh.

SCRAWDYKE: Then make y' way t' t' Gates café. Me an' Nipple'll foller y' at a distance, casually, an' join y' there. We'll 'ave a cup o' tea an' we'll keep a lookout through t' winder. (*They sit down.*)

WICK: We'll be able t' see Irwin when 'e turns t' corner of East Parade an' goes in t' studio. Triumph.

SCRAWDYKE: But we mustn't show it.

WICK: No play it dead cool man.

SCRAWDYKE: We mustn't mention it. Talk about something else.

WICK: Is pickin' one's nose a venial or a mortal sin? If one postulates the Deity as a Super Stick Insect where does that place the average man?

51

SCRAWDYKE: We sup up. Come on 'ere, an' that's it.
(They get up.)
WICK: In the bag!
SCRAWDYKE: The first phase completed.
WICK: Gone without an 'itch.
SCRAWDYKE: We've done it!
(WICK shakes hands with SCRAWDYKE.)
WICK: Congratulations.
SCRAWDYKE: Well done!
(They all shake hands with each other.)
NIPPLE: Hee hee.
SCRAWDYKE: Well done Irwin.
INGHAM: Oh—well—ta.
(They walk round each other, shaking hands, patting one another on the back.)
WICK: Master stroke.
SCRAWDYKE: Well done lads.
NIPPLE: Hee hee.
SCRAWDYKE: Great, great.
WICK: Went like clockwork.
SCRAWDYKE: Yeh.
(The congratulations peter out. They are left standing there. Pause.)
WICK: It'll be a doddle.
SCRAWDYKE: Without question. Right. Now we've got the paintin' 'ere we move on t' t' next phase.
WICK: Gettin' Allard!
INGHAM: 'Ow d' y' suggest we do that?
NIPPLE: Put 'im in a taxi.
SCRAWDYKE: Got it! 'Is own car!
(Pulls bed into position for car.)
Right we wait be'ind the fence 'ere. Just by the gap. Allard's car's parked just along, there.
WICK: We wear masks.

(*Gets out handkerchief.*)
Round our mouths.
(SCRAWDYKE *hasn't got a hanky. He finds a brightly coloured bit of rag.*)

INGHAM: I 'aven't got a——

SCRAWDYKE: Use a rag then.

INGHAM: Oh yeh.

NIPPLE: Where's one for me?

SCRAWDYKE: I don't know—use that.

NIPPLE: Err, this?

SCRAWDYKE: Yes, get it on.

NIPPLE: Errgh, it somebody's mucky old vest.

SCRAWDYKE: Well get it on!

NIPPLE: I'n't there anything else?

SCRAWDYKE: Stop quibbling an' get it on.

NIPPLE: Waargh.

WICK: So we're in be'ind the fence.

SCRAWDYKE: Yes. Come on, Nipple.

NIPPLE: Aar A c'n 'ardly breathe in this smelly thing.

WICK: It's great. It looks very sinister.

SCRAWDYKE: We've all got sticks.
(*He grabs sticks, bits of wood, and hands them out.*)
Right, now Allard comes out of the buildin'.
(WICK *runs off to be Allard, pulling off the handkerchief, dropping stick.*)
We wait, just by the openin' in the fence, like a coiled spring ready t' pounce.

WICK: Allard comes out of the Tech. Just as 'e always does. Feelin' cheerful an' a little tired, thinkin' about 'is supper, 'is wife, an' 'is bed.

SCRAWDYKE: 'Ummin' to 'imself. Lookin' forward to a nice drive 'ome through the snow.

53

WICK: Thinkin' about all the little things 'at 'ave
'appened durin' the day. The little kicks.
When 'e told a joke in the staff room, the
warm feelin' 'e got when ev'rybody
chuckled. The little annoyances 'e's 'ad like
catchin' students chuckin' clay at the
model.

SCRAWDYKE: But all in all it's been a good day.

WICK: An unexceptionable day.

SCRAWDYKE: But a good day.

(WICK *starts walking, humming to himself.*)

WICK: 'E walks down the side of the Tech. Turns
the corner into St. Paul's Street.

SCRAWDYKE: Goes past the gap an' gets to 'is car.

WICK: 'E gets out 'is keys.

SCRAWDYKE: Bends down to open the door. We come
out, quickly, from the darkness, silently.
(WICK *starts to unbend but they are on him.*
SCRAWDYKE *leading. They rain pretend blows
down on him. After the initial few blows all
the assailants seem to get carried away by
what they are doing:* WICK *lets out muffled
gasps and groans. Finally* WICK *lies inert.*
SCRAWDYKE *gives him a final kick and they
have finished.*)

NIPPLE: Ah, ah, we've killed 'im, hee, hee.

SCRAWDYKE: No! Get 'im in the car.
(*They seize hold of* WICK *and heave him into
the "back seat".*)
Irwin, the wheel, Nipple in the back.
(SCRAWDYKE *sits beside* INGHAM.)
Start 'er up!

INGHAM: Oh—er—well.

SCRAWDYKE: Ignition!

INGHAM: Oh yeh.
(WICK *raises himself up.*)

WICK: Are we goin' to reverse?

INGHAM: Oh look, A mean, let's not.

SCRAWDYKE: No attract too much attention. Straight on St. Paul's.

WICK: Mmmmmmmmmmmm . . .

NIPPLE: Stop at the end.

SCRAWDYKE: Straight round the corner.

WICK: MMMmmm, up past Sparrer Park, Mmm . . .
(*When he isn't speaking and the car is moving* WICK *makes MMMM noise.*)

SCRAWDYKE: Stop at the traffic lights.

NIPPLE: There aren't any traffic lights there.

SCRAWDYKE: There are.

WICK: Crash straight ahead through 'em.

SCRAWDYKE: Too risky.

NIPPLE: They've changed.

SCRAWDYKE: Not yet— They've changed!

WICK: Straight up Ramsden Street.

SCRAWDYKE: Yeh.

WICK: Up t' the top.

SCRAWDYKE: No not up t' t' main street. Too many people. Turn on Peel Street.

NIPPLE: Hee hee, past t' Police Station.

WICK: No we don't want that. Reverse.

INGHAM: Ooh!

WICK: Reverse Irwin, quick, quick. The's a cop lookin' at us.

SCRAWDYKE: Back int' Ramsden Street again.

NIPPLE: Which way a' we goin'?

WICK: Back down t' t' crossroads an' on Queen's Street.

SCRAWDYKE: No, no. That's past Tech. They'll all be comin' out.

WICK: We'll 'ave t' go back then, back t' St. Paul's an' go on the other way.

SCRAWDYKE: Back where we started!

INGHAM: No, no the's another little street like off
Ramsden Street, top side o' t' Town 'All,
A don't know its name.

NIPPLE: Aye there is. Back o' Whitfields shop.

SCRAWDYKE: On there then.

WICK: Not many about.

NIPPLE: Their dark car speeds through unknowin'
snowflecked streets of night.

SCRAWDYKE: Turn down Princess Street.

WICK: Then on Alfred Street.

SCRAWDYKE: Then up East Parade.

WICK: Look out for that lorry Skreeetch! Phew!
That was a close one!

NIPPLE: Door's come open.

SCRAWDYKE: Close it!

WICK: Allard's fallen out!

SCRAWDYKE: Can't 'ave. Round the corner. Pull up.
(*Short pause.*)

WICK: Man what a ride!

SCRAWDYKE: O.K. now is there anything about?

NIPPLE: The's a trolley comin' up Chapel 'Ill.

SCRAWDYKE: Never mind. We'll get 'im out. It's only a
couple o' yards in t' t' buildin'. If anybody
interferes we'll say 'e's drunk.

WICK: My father, madam. Don't y' think it's
amazing I've turned out so well?
(*He lies down.*)

SCRAWDYKE: All right get 'old of 'im. That end Irwin,
come on.

NIPPLE: Ai want to take me rag off.

WICK: Don't be disgustin'.

SCRAWDYKE: Right, get 'im upright. Under 'is arms,
come on. Across the pavement. Ugh. An' in
at the door. Now we've got t' get 'im up
these bloody stairs.

56

WICK: Well look we've got the real stairs just outside. Why don't we——

SCRAWDYKE: Aye. Good idea. Come on.
(*They all go out of the door and close it behind them. We can only hear them. They run down to the bottom of the stairs.*)

WICK: Oo still snowin'! Man it's cold!

SCRAWDYKE: Right get 'old of 'im again. Other side Nipple. Irwin what a' you doin'?

INGHAM: Be'ind.

SCRAWDYKE: O.K. let's—ugh— Come on! Push Irwin.

INGHAM: I am.

NIPPLE: Yoo're not takin' enough weight.

SCRAWDYKE: I am, you aren't.

NIPPLE: Ai can't take any more.

SCRAWDYKE: 'Course y' can.

NIPPLE: Yoo don't know 'ow t' lift.

SCRAWDYKE: I'm bearin' the brunt. Anybody c'n see you've never carried——

NIPPLE: Now, y've got y' arms all wrong. They should be like this.

SCRAWDYKE: Don't let go! Aargh! Y've pinned me against the wall y' silly bastard!

NIPPLE: Noe Ai 'av'n't, you've done it.

WICK: Wait a jiff A'll stand on me own weight a bit.

SCRAWDYKE: Oh! Right, get 'im, under this way.

NIPPLE: Noe y' can't.

SCRAWDYKE: Do as y' told.

NIPPLE: It's not——

SCRAWDYKE: Shurrup and lift.
(*Measured tread of somebody descending stairs from above studio.* INGHAM *whispers.*)

INGHAM: The's somebody comin'!
(*They talk urgently in whispers. Measured tread continues down.*)

57

WICK: From t' top floor!

INGHAM: Go back down.

SCRAWDYKE: No stay as we are.

NIPPLE: 'E won't be able t' get past.

SCRAWDYKE: Yes 'e c'n squeeze, press against the wall.

NIPPLE: But what——

SCRAWDYKE: Shhh!

(*Footsteps continue. Then stop as* WICK *says:*)

WICK: Huh, slipped outside, sprained me ankle.

SCRAWDYKE: 'E'll be all right when we get 'im inside.

WICK: Yeh, just twisted it really—huh.

(*Pause. Footsteps start down again.*)

SCRAWDYKE: Come on lads let's get 'im up there. Not far now. Lift Nipple.

NIPPLE: Ai am.

SCRAWDYKE: Nearly— Ugh—just a bit——

(*Door opens. They come in lugging* WICK. SCRAWDYKE *at one side*, NIPPLE *at the other*, INGHAM *behind*.)

Put 'im on t' bed.

(*They get him on to the bed.*)

'E was a weird bloke. Never said anything, just stared. What was the matter with 'im? We told a plausible story, did it convincingly. Most people would 'ave sympathized. 'E was an odd bastard. What— Tah! The masks! We still 'ad the bloody masks on!

(WICK *laughs on bed.*)

NIPPLE: Aar yoo ought to 'ave thought of that.

SCRAWDYKE: What about you? You didn't realize.

NIPPLE: Ah but yoo're supposed t' be the Leader.

SCRAWDYKE: Well never mind. It doesn't matter. 'E probably thought we were playin' some kind of game, just playin' around. Let's get

58

on. Allard's unconscious on the bed. We
'ave the paintin' facin' 'im for when 'e
comes round.
(*He places an old canvas on an easel in the
required position.*)
An' we all stand ready. Me in the middle.
Irwin there, Wick'll be there, an' Nipple
there.

NIPPLE: Are we just goin' t' wait for 'im t' come
round? It could tek hours.

SCRAWDYKE: No. Irwin'll chuck some water over 'is
'ead.

INGHAM: Oh, what——

SCRAWDYKE: In that jug.

INGHAM: Oh it's full.

WICK: Ey, 'e's not goin' to——

SCRAWDYKE: No just reckon Irwin, just reckon.
(INGHAM *makes a vague gesture with the jug
in* WICK'S *direction.*)
Now back in position. Our sticks.
(*He collects the stick.* INGHAM *puts down the
jug. They resume position. The three of them
stand there, masked, their sticks raised
menacingly. Slowly* WICK *begins to move and
groan, then he very dazedly raises his head a
little, wipes his hand across his eyes, then
peers at the three. When at last he seems to
have got them into focus,* SCRAWDYKE *says:*)
Good evening, Mr. Allard!

NIPPLE: I'm going t' t' bog.
(NIPPLE *goes out.*)

SCRAWDYKE: Why did you seduce Margaret Thwaite?

WICK: Margaret Thwaite?

SCRAWDYKE: Please don't weary us by denying it.

WICK: 'E's beginning to regain consciousness. 'Is
cunnin' little brain's beginnin' t' work.

SCRAWDYKE: We must expect it. After the first shock.
We mustn't underestimate 'im.

WICK: What proof have you?

SCRAWDYKE: Ah so you admit there is something to be
proved.

WICK: I didn't say that.

SCRAWDYKE: That's what you implied.

WICK: Look here, Scrawdyke, what are your
terms of reference?

SCRAWDYKE: My eyes. The eyes of my comrades. The
testimony of the girl herself.

WICK: Now look here Scrawdyke suppose I admit
that——

SCRAWDYKE: Suppose nothing. I deal in facts. And if
those aren't enough for you I need only
mention——

WICK: What?

SCRAWDYKE: Eric Tomlinson.
(WICK'S *mouth falls open, his eyes roll, he
gasps for air.*)
Water!

INGHAM: In 'is face?

SCRAWDYKE: To drink.
(INGHAM *runs to sink, brings cup to* WICK
*who seizes it, gulps down the water, then
lies on his back panting.*)

WICK: Ah, ah, ah, ah, ah,—but 'ow—'ow, oh no,
ah, ah——

SCRAWDYKE: But surely Mr. Allard you must 'ave
suspected all along that I knew?

WICK: Oh, oh, ah, ah, my—oh, ah, oh—
(*Slowly* WICK *sits up and brings himself to
speak.*)
All right Scrawdyke—I admit there is
something in what you say—you're
perfectly correct in your assumption that I

60

did suspect you knew—but I could never be sure, and as time went on I began to imagine—I see now that I committed a major blunder in dismissing you. Yes you've got me. I seriously underestimated you. You've proved more than a match for me. God you're clever.

SCRAWDYKE: I'll grant you that. That's one point on which we agree.

WICK: Listen, Scrawdyke, I'm a reasonable man, let bygones be bygones, you can all return to the school.

(SCRAWDYKE *ostentatiously turns away, yawns.*)

I'll get you better grants!

SCRAWDYKE: The British Centipedes fall into three orders. Those having 15 body-segments, those having 22 body-segments, and those having 31 to 173 body-segments. Did you know that Irwin?

INGHAM: Er—no.

WICK: I'll make sure you all get N.D.D.!

SCRAWDYKE: It's a fact.

WICK: I can do it, I have influence, I can pull strings!

(SCRAWDYKE *walks about humming to himself.*)

I'll get you into the Slade, Royal College, Rome Scholarship.

(SCRAWDYKE *looks out of the window, his back to* WICK.)

I'll appoint you deputy headmaster. I can fix it with higher authority. I have money, you can have it. My daughter, she's lovely, she's ripe, I——

(SCRAWDYKE *suddenly turns.*)

61

SCRAWDYKE: I don't want your daughter! I don't want your money! I don't want your jobs! I don't want your scholarships!

WICK: Then what do you want?

SCRAWDYKE: I want you!

(*Pause.*)

WICK: What——

SCRAWDYKE: I want you, in my power, utterly and completely! I want you to surrender every last vestige of self-respect to me. I want you to throw your worthless life on my mercy. I want you to give yourself completely into my keeping. I want to 'ollow you out and fill you in with nothing but 'umiliation. I want you to destroy yourself as a man in front of me. 'Ere. Now. In this room. Then I want t' see you crawl away an' cringe out the rest of y'r days in my shadow. I want you to become my excreta.

(WICK *sits stunned. Then suddenly, like a wild animal, he leaps up and hurls himself at the door. He pulls at it frantically, then, finding it won't open, he starts to pound on it frenziedly.* SCRAWDYKE *looks on unmoving, unsmiling.* INGHAM *watches alarmed. As* WICK'S *strength ebbs he sinks towards the floor, his blows get weaker. Finally he is a whimpering heap on the floor.*)

Pull y'self together man. I expected better of you.

(SCRAWDYKE *gestures to* INGHAM *to drag* WICK *over and prop him against the radio cabinet.* INGHAM *does this.* WICK *is completely unresistant, an inert mass.*)

Listen! Are y' listenin'?

62

(WICK *whimpers weakly*.)

WICK: Yeaas.

SCRAWDYKE: You see this painting?

(*He moves easel to central position.*)

D' y' know what it is? I'll tell you what it is. It's one of the world's greatest masterpieces. Garden at Cookham Rise by Stanley Spencer.

WICK: But——

SCRAWDYKE: Never mind how we got it. It's 'ere, we're 'ere, an' so are you. That's all that matters. Full cast and props for the drama t' be enacted. It's very simple. In return for your smashing this painting we give you our silence. In return for your integrity we give you back your career.

WICK: But, but—how do I know——

SCRAWDYKE: 'Ow d' y' know we won't split on you after all? Y' don't. Y'll just 'ave t' trust us. An emotion you're not very familiar with. But y'll 'ave to try it. Just a little simple 'uman trust Philip. We aren't all as black as you. Just put your trust in us, relax, let y'self go, have faith. For the first time in your life 'ave a little faith.

WICK: I have no alternative. And—and I think you're a man of your word.

SCRAWDYKE: Good. 'Elp Mr. Allard to 'is feet Irwin.

INGHAM: Oh—yeh.

(INGHAM *helps* WICK *up.* WICK *stands tottering before the painting.* SCRAWDYKE *gets a hammer, he holds it out to* WICK *who hesitates then takes it.* WICK *raises it and stands swaying in front of the painting. Pause. Then suddenly he smashes savagely at the canvas, ripping into it. His attack grows*

63

more furious with every blow. SCRAWDYKE
eggs him on and INGHAM *starts to grin
maliciously.* SCRAWDYKE *starts to chant then*
INGHAM *joins in.*)

SCRAWDYKE: Smash it! Smash it! Smash it! Smash it!
Smash it! Smash it . . .

INGHAM: Smash it! Yes. Smash it! Smash it——
(WICK *hurls the painting from the easel and
hits, tramples, snaps and tears at it on the
floor until finally he is kicking and stamping
on a twisted wreck. He comes to a standstill,
exhausted. The chanting dies. They all stand
motionless staring at the wreck. Then*
SCRAWDYKE *goes over to* WICK, *bends close
to his ear, and whispers.*)

SCRAWDYKE: Your trust was misplaced.
(WICK *looks up.*)
Now we 'ave ev'rything. Integrity and
career.

BLACKOUT

SCENE 4

Later the same afternoon. It is somewhat darker, as the scene proceeds the daylight fades, going through the grey-blue of snowy winter dusk until, by the last part of the scene, it is dark outside and SCRAWDYKE *and* WICK *are talking in almost complete darkness, there only being the last vestiges of light coming in through the window.* INGHAM *is painting the banner—*SCRAWDYKE *and* WICK *are sitting.* NIPPLE *enters.*

WICK: Aha 'ere it is.

SCRAWDYKE: Y've been t' the gallery?

NIPPLE: Mm.

WICK: Y've checked up on the size of the paintin's?

NIPPLE: Let me tell y'.

SCRAWDYKE: All right give us y'r report.

NIPPLE: —Ai left where Ai live in Spaines Road an' boarded a trolley, Ai knew that what was normally a short prosaic journey was t' be mutated by the magic wand of winter into an odyssey through the 'aunted chasms of perpetual day—night. Ai 'ave a very strong sense of these things. Through the wintry ghostlight of the snow the machine wove sluggishly its pre-ordained way along the destiny written with wire for it in the sky above. Seemin'ly completely in its power, as if Ai and not it, were the prisoner, Ai 'uddled shoulder t' shoulder with mai fellow-travellers, inert as if 'ibernatin',

65

givin' out nothing, yet quick an' alive mai
sense of mission lurked passionately within
the depths of mai skull. Aaaah—
Well, we got as far as that church, y' know,
at t' bottom o' Wheat'ouse Road, an' a car
'ad skidded madly across the road in front
of us, blockin' the way. The machine
churned wearily to a standstill. Ai wrenched
maiself from its shelter an' began to trudge
through the snows of an 'Uddersfield-made
Siberia. Men moved like Eskimos about
me, an' Ai could feel as Ai——

SCRAWDYKE: So you walked to the gallery. Did y' get
the measurements?

NIPPLE: Wait until A tell y'.

SCRAWDYKE: We 'av'n't time. The putsch is scheduled
for next Friday not 1969.

WICK: We asked y' for a report not a fifteen-
volume prose poem.

NIPPLE: Waah——

SCRAWDYKE: Did y' get the measurements?

NIPPLE: Yes.

WICK: Give 'em 'ere.

(NIPPLE *gets a crumpled bit of paper out of
his pocket*.)

Ta.

SCRAWDYKE: Did y' check up on 'ow the paintin's are
'ung?

NIPPLE: Yes. It's 'ow we said.

WICK: Any of 'em'll go in that portfolio.

SCRAWDYKE: Good.

WICK: Let's 'ave some tea.

(WICK *fills kettle, lights gas, puts kettle on,
puts tea in pot, etc*.)

NIPPLE: On me way 'ere from t' gallery Ai saw
somebody yoo know.

66

SCRAWDYKE: 'Oo?

NIPPLE: One o' t' girls from t' Art School.

SCRAWDYKE: That could be any one o' fifty.

NIPPLE: Noe, noe, this's a partic'lar one. One yoo fancy.

SCRAWDYKE: What d' y' mean I fancy?

NIPPLE: Y' know which one Ai mean, what's 'er name? Ann. Ann something——

WICK: Graves, Finley?

NIPPLE: Noe.

WICK: Ann Spencer, Anne Daniels——

NIPPLE: No it's not that.

WICK: Ann Gedge. Anne Waddington. Anne——

NIPPLE: That's it, y' just——

SCRAWDYKE: I never fancied Anne Waddington!

NIPPLE: No, not 'er, the one y' said before.

WICK: Gedge?

NIPPLE: Yes that's the one.

WICK: A never knew y' 'ad a yen for 'er Mal.

SCRAWDYKE: I didn't. 'E's in another of 'is fantasies.

NIPPLE: Oh but y' do, y' told me, y' went on about the nape of 'er neck.

WICK: Haha, a nape fetishist.

SCRAWDYKE: I never said anything about the nape of 'er neck.

NIPPLE: Oh y' did. Y' went on and on about it. About its slope an' the little groove in it.

SCRAWDYKE: I never said anything . . . I don't go round lookin' for grooves in girls' necks. That's one of your perversions. I may 'ave made some general remark about 'er, she's not a bad-lookin' lass from what I remember. Though A'm not sure I'm thinkin' about the one you're talkin' about. There are so many birds down in that place, they're all alike.

NIPPLE: Noe——

WICK: I know 'er, I 'ad a session with 'er once. Durin' that dance we 'ad last year she got me t' tek 'er outside an'— Well, a right little virgin she turned out t' be. Y' know scared stiff. Yeh she's a— Anyway A just got browned off.

NIPPLE: Ai c'n always tell when a woman's ready to go. It's a matter of intuition. A mysterious chemical combination drawin' y' together.

WICK: Is that so.

NIPPLE: Women respond t' me, they sense— something in me. Ai wish Ai 'ad a shillin' for all the girls Ai've been out with. Ai seem t' attract ev'ry sort from shy little shop assistants t' darin' intellectual women. Ai 'ave this certain inner magnet which pulls 'em towards me. They sense the pristine animal in me, hee hee. It's ev'ry age group as well. Even married women with kids are drawn towards mee. Their reason tries t' struggle but it's futile, they finally abandon themselves an' lose themselves— Sometimes Ai try t' restrain meself, knowin' the 'avoc Ai'll wreak in these women's lives. But it's no use, Ai 'ave t' give in t' the ineluctable—suckin' force within me. The 'ole fabric of these women's lives is cast away for one savage moment of ecstasy. One woman can't satisfy me for long an' Ai 'ave t' move on. Ai just can't 'elp meself— There was this woman at this party. She was the wife of some jazz musician 'oo'd come over from Leeds. She 'ad Negro blood in 'er, y' know, y' could tell. She 'ad this dark pigmented skin and these untamed eyes, these sensual thick fleshy lips. She 'ad these 'eavy heavin' breasts, a narrer waist, an' great rounded fecund 'ips that she swung provocatively ev'ry time she moved. She 'ad this taut dress on an' nothing underneath—Ai found that out later. It was as tight as a drum-skin an' y' could see ev'ry sensual tremor in 'er body. She moved with this rhythm like a black she-panther. Aaaaah— Well when Ai got there she was by 'erself like at one side. She seemed t' be detached from it all, bored and caged in by all the pale in'ibited males from this area 'oo surrounded 'er. Then she saw me! An' there was this immediate recognition, this sexual spark flashed between us! Our eyes mated. She was transformed— Well, A thought, Ai'll let things take their natural course. Ai'll let 'er come to me, Ai won't make it too easy for 'er, Ai'll let 'er 'unt me down. So Ai got a drink an' chatted t' people over the other side of the room. Not lookin' at 'er but sensin' all the time 'er presence, comin' nearer, bein' drawn ineluctably. Sure enough Ai turn an' there she is, sort of tremblin' by me side. We didn't speak. There was no need for mundane words. Before we knew it we were clasped together pulsatin'. Pulsatin' t' the music in a crazy primordeal frenzy. Our mouths gnawed 'ungrily at each other. 'Er thick fleshy 'ot lips engulfed me. Our tongues conversed with a wet, wanton wildness, writhin' an' twistin' like angry snakes. She suddenly bit into me tongue,

69

sinkin' 'er teeth in, the spasm of pain shot through me. But it wasn't a pain like an ordinary pain. It was an ecstatic flame 'at lept through mai innards makin' 'em throb an' glow. Before Ai knew it we were upstairs in a bedroom. An' she—she'd unzipped me! An' she 'ad mai—she 'ad it in 'er 'and! An' she was squeezin'. An' she said: "Do anything to me. 'Urt me. Tear me. Tear me. Make me feel." An' I sez, Ai sez, Ai sez: "What d' y' want me t' do?" An' she starts rippin' at me, tearin' me clo'es off, clawin' off me shirt, wrenchin' off me pants. An' Ai'm tearing off 'er frock, an' we fall, tearin' on the bed. An' we fuse together in t' one white 'ot furnace of fusion— An' Ai c'n 'ear the toms toms of 'er ancestors drummin' in me ears, in me blood, in me thighs— An' ev'rything's obliterated. 'Uddersfield dissolves, Yorkshire disappears. The twentieth century—the's only this moment, this act of pure savage elemental being. There in that room. Just this furnace. Just this energy. Just this——

(*Pause.*)

WICK: Just one question.

NIPPLE: Ai never saw 'er again.

WICK: What was the record y' danced to?

NIPPLE: What a woman! She was a woman 'at even Ai could 'ave gone with more than once.

WICK: Bit 'eavy on clothes though.

NIPPLE: 'Oo cares about shirts.

WICK: Very true. Next time she comes over let me know. A've got a couple of old shirts she's quite welcome t' rip off me. D' y' think A

70

should wear two shirts t' prolong the
ecstasy?

(*The water should be boiling about here.*
WICK *makes the tea. During the following
conversation they all get themselves some.*)
Well Irwin, 'ow did y' like the sound o'
that then.

INGHAM: Oh well—aye—it sounded—int'restin'.

WICK: Y' see y've got 'im int'rested. Y' shouldn't
go tellin' stories like that in front of Irwin
'ere. 'E won't 'ave any time for 'is raffia
work now. 'E'll be runnin' round
'Uddersfield lookin' for Negro women wi'
drum-tight skirts an' untamed eyes. 'E
won't rest until 'e's 'eard them tom toms.
The's goin' to be a nasty incident on a
corporation trolley. Y'd better walk 'ome
from now on Irwin. We don't want war
wi' Jamaica.

NIPPLE: Hee hee.

SCRAWDYKE: There's just one thing y' forgot t' mention.

NIPPLE: What?

SCRAWDYKE: I was at that party.

NIPPLE: Y' weren't.

SCRAWDYKE: I was. It was up at 'Arry Sutton's.

WICK: Ey, y' saw this primordeal sex goddess?

SCRAWDYKE: I saw 'er. A pale, skinny little kid with a
spotty face an' a slight squint. 'Er eyes
were untamed all right, she couldn't focus
'em. An' as for a drumtight skirt, if y'd
made a frock for 'er out of an 'andkerchief,
it'd 'ave 'ung like a tent. If she didn't wear
underwear it was because she didn't need
to. 'Er chances of bein' bothered were less
than nil until this pristine animal arrived
on t' scene. Y' know, she was the only bird

71

left, an' even then, desperate as she was, it was an 'ard job for the Memoirs of Casanova t' make 'er. Even though she was a beggar she was still a bit choosy.

NIPPLE: You weren't there.

WICK: So it was all a big fib Nipple.

NIPPLE: Waargh. Ai'm goin' for a pee.

WICK: Tell us all about it when y' come back. I'm in the mood for a good adventure story.

(NIPPLE *goes out. We hear feet plodding upstairs.*)

What a deluded——!

SCRAWDYKE: Yeh. Let's 'ave some more tea.

(*He gets himself some tea.* WICK *goes and looks at* INGHAM.)

WICK: 'Ow's it goin'?

INGHAM: Oh—A've nearly finished.

WICK: Yeh. It's great. It'll look good unfurled above us as we march. The symbol of Dynamic Erection.

SCRAWDYKE: Aye.

(*Footsteps.* NIPPLE *comes in.*)

NIPPLE: Ai'm off now. Ai want t' get on with some work.

SCRAWDYKE: Well shut the bloody door it's freezin'.

WICK: Ah, y're goin' off t' slave over an 'ot page. To add a few more tellin' paragraphs to the Novel of the Twentieth Century.

NIPPLE: Mm.

WICK: 'Ow far've y' got with it now?

NIPPLE: Well Ai'm still werkin' on the first movement.

WICK: 'Ow many chapters?

NIPPLE: It doesn't 'ave chapters. It just 'as these movements.

72

WICK: T' first movement plods, t' second movement stands still, and t' third movement drops dead.

NIPPLE: 'Ow would yoo know, y've not read it.

WICK: No but I've 'eard you talk about it. Indeed I'll go further, I've 'eard you talk it.

NIPPLE: Waah.

WICK: Tell me, is the rumour true that you and your novel are one and the same? Or are you just good friends?

NIPPLE: What d' y'——?

WICK: Y've been talkin' this novel ever since A met y'. You're a case of a man written by a book.

NIPPLE: Err, very funny. Just becos Ai 'ave a gift for verbal——

WICK: That stuff about the Negress, A bet that's goin' in.

NIPPLE: Maybee.

WICK: Am I goin' in?

NIPPLE: Noe.

WICK: But I'm a very int'restin' character.

NIPPLE: Ai don't deel in characters.

WICK: Well what do y' deal in?

NIPPLE: The quest. The quest for the reel be'ind the tawdry panoply of seemin'——

WICK: A Western?

NIPPLE: —Ai like t' think of it as a metaphysical strip show.

WICK: That sounds a bit near the knuckle. It doesn't sound like the kind of book I'd let my maid read.

NIPPLE: It won't be an easy werk t' grasp. Ai make demands.

WICK: What's it called?

NIPPLE: From Out The Cocoon.

WICK: Portrait Of The Artist As A Young Bug.

NIPPLE: Ah well Ai'm not goin' t' bandy words. It's unworthy of me. When's the next meetin'?

SCRAWDYKE: Tomorra afternoon.

NIPPLE: What time?

SCRAWDYKE: About two.

WICK: Scrawdyke the Fourth tomorra.

NIPPLE: Well A'll see y'.

WICK: S'long.

INGHAM: Aye, s'long.

(*He goes.*)

WICK: What a nutter!

SCRAWDYKE: 'E's not a person 'e's an absurdity.

WICK: 'E's never 'ad owt published?

SCRAWDYKE: 'As 'e 'eck. 'E lives on National Assistance.

INGHAM: Well A've finished this now like Mal. It just needs t' dry like.

WICK: Y've done a bloody good job Irwin.

SCRAWDYKE: It'll do.

INGHAM: Aye, well A think A'd better be off an' all now. That is unless o' course——

WICK: Ah y've got an assignation wi' one o' these Negresses 'ave y'?

INGHAM: Nay A wish A 'ad.

WICK: Just one o' these pale pelted 'Uddersfield beauties is it? Wi' breasts n' bigger'n bee stings.

INGHAM: No it's just me tea.

WICK: 'Ow y' goin' t' 'andle y' mam?

INGHAM: Well like A'll 'ave t' some'ow make 'er think like 'at, well, 'at A'm considerin' goin' back—A mean not 'at I er—but anyway. Until A move in 'ere. Ooh it's not goin' t' be easy. A'm not lookin' forward to it.

SCRAWDYKE: Just do it.

INGHAM: Aye. Well A'm off then.

SCRAWDYKE: O.K.

INGHAM: Oh—er—like, Mal.

WICK: A thought y'd decided t' go?

INGHAM: I 'ave but— Well A was goin' t' say—A
mean what A was goin' t' say was well A
thought like—A mean unless you 'ave
some other— Well, anyway A thought like
A might well, pop, y' know just pop, up t'
t' Jazz Club for an hour or so t'night. Y'
know if the's nothing 'at——

SCRAWDYKE: It costs two bob t' get in t' that Jazz Club.
We need ev'ry penny we've got for the
struggle. We can't squander.

INGHAM: Aye A know Mal. But A thought like A
might be able t' get in for nowt. Y' know
if the's somebody 'oo knows me like on t'
door.

SCRAWDYKE: Nah. I know you. If they ask y' t' pay, y'
will.

INGHAM: Oh all right a'm off.

SCRAWDYKE: Don't go near that Jazz Club.

INGHAM: Right. S'long.

(INGHAM *goes*.)

WICK: A wu'n't mind goin' up t' that Jazz Club
meself.

SCRAWDYKE: Aye, well we will.

WICK: Aha.

SCRAWDYKE: I can always get in for nothing. In fact
they usually refuse t' take my money even
if I offer it. I know 'em all, Keith Smith,
Archy, Trevor Kaye, Selwyn, Mike Clay. I
introduced most of 'em t' Jazz in t' first
place. I was probably the first person in
this town to understand what Jazz is.

WICK: Oh aye they all know me an' all. You an'

75

me an' one or two others are jazz in this
town.

SCRAWDYKE: Yeh.

WICK: A wonder when Selwyn's goin' t' come for
that drum?

SCRAWDYKE: D'know. It's been 'ere three weeks.

WICK: Aye, well 'e's usin' that other.

SCRAWDYKE: That one he?

WICK: Yeh.

SCRAWDYKE: Anyway we'll go. It'll be a shrewd move. If
we appear there just as usual nobody'll
suspect owt.

WICK: Aye we must be'ave as if nothin's
'appenin'. If we don't go they'll start——

SCRAWDYKE: We've got to go.

WICK: We can't avoid it.
(*Pause.*)
Well it's not snowin' at the moment. Foo
but it's cold. Seems t' be gettin' colder.
That stupid little thing's been on all day
an' it's still freezin'. Ha but we're goin' t'
warm things up next Friday!

SCRAWDYKE: Aye. Put that Gerry Mulligan on.

WICK: Yes that's just what we need.
(WICK *puts on* "*Frenesi*" *by the original
Gerry Mulligan Quartet.*)

SCRAWDYKE: This's just the weather for our conspiracy.
Y' need extreme weather as a background
to extreme action. It 'eightens it. Gives it
an epic quality. Great 'eat or great cold.
That's what y' need.

WICK: Mild days are for mild men. The average
temperature's for the average man.

SCRAWDYKE: Yeh.

WICK: It was snowin' in Petrograd.

SCRAWDYKE: Mussolini marched on Rome in an 'eat

76

wave.

WICK: It was blazin' in Sarajevo when Princip let 'im 'ave it.

SCRAWDYKE: January 1933 was the coldest January for fifteen years.

WICK: Was it?

SCRAWDYKE: Yes.

WICK: A wonder if it was as cold as this?

SCRAWDYKE: It wasn't.

WICK: That's a good omen. Friday, Scrawdyke the Ninth, Year One. It's going t' be our October Revolution, our Easter Week, our July 20th, our Burning of the Reichstag, our——

SCRAWDYKE: Our Conquest of Mexico.

WICK: A say, Mal, between you an' me, when we get t' power, what are goin' t' be our aims, A mean our real aims? What a' we goin' t' do with it?

SCRAWDYKE: Between ourselves?

WICK: Yeh.

SCRAWDYKE: Nothing!

WICK: Nothing?

SCRAWDYKE: We want power purely for its own sake.

WICK: To enjoy it.

SCRAWDYKE: We shan't pursue any specific policy for its intrinsic value.

WICK: What we do with it doesn't matter.

SCRAWDYKE: In that sense we shall do nothing.

WICK: But there'll be plenty activity.

SCRAWDYKE: Purely arbitrary activity.

WICK: Perverse activity.

SCRAWDYKE: Strictly for giggles.

WICK: Our giggles.

SCRAWDYKE: The Absurd State.

WICK: Absurdity with vengeance.

SCRAWDYKE: Naked unadorned vengeance. Ten thousand years of culture will be given into our hands, for our safe-keeping, and we will let it fall, shattering it completely.

WICK: And the Bomb?

SCRAWDYKE: Drop it.

WICK: Of course.

SCRAWDYKE: Cruelty.

WICK: For its own sake.

SCRAWDYKE: No excuses. Our whim, that will be morality.

WICK: The freedom of the one demands the servitude of the many.

SCRAWDYKE: Which is what they really desire.

WICK: Which is what they crave.

SCRAWDYKE: We shall rear up our soaring pyramids dedicated to nothing. The millions will climb the steps in pain to vanish at the top. Agony will be the order of our new day. If you ask me for Justice I will punch you in the mouth. If you ask me for Mercy I will kick you in the balls! If you ask me for Love I will knock you to the ground. And if you ask me for Truth, I will show you my fist, my boot and my laughing face!

WICK: (*quietly*). The Final Solution of the Human Question.

(*Music stops.*)

BLACKOUT

78

SCENE 5

*The boom, boom, boom, of a drum. Lights up. It is dark
outside. The four are marching round the room in a tight
formation.* SCRAWDYKE *is slightly ahead, by his side* WICK
carries the banner. Behind them march INGHAM, *banging the
drum, and* NIPPLE. *All except* INGHAM *have their arms raised
in the party salute. They go round the room once, twice.*
NIPPLE *begins to lag behind a tiny bit. They go round a third
time.*

WICK: We arrive at the Market Cross.
> (*They line up in front of the table.* INGHAM
> *changes rhythm to a slower beat.* WICK *runs
> to tape recorder and switches on an anthem,
> "Laudation". Then he resumes his position in
> the line.* SCRAWDYKE *walks gravely down the
> line, inspecting and shaking hands with each
> one in turn, starting off with a couple of
> phantom members. When he gets to* NIPPLE
> *he adjusts his duffle coat as if it is a uniform
> slightly out of order.*)

NIPPLE: Waa——
> (SCRAWDYKE *mounts the table by means of
> the radio cabinet.* WICK *moves to the tape
> recorder and switches it on.* SCRAWDYKE
> *stands saluting. Mass crowd cheers resound
> from the recorder.* WICK *fades them off and
> mounts the radio cabinet which is just by
> him.*)

WICK: Malcolm Scrawdyke. On behalf of the

79

Party, on behalf of the Nation, I address
you. At this critical moment in world
history I call upon you. You, and you
alone, are our saviour. You are the
Supreme Embodiment of all that is finest
in Human Nature. You are the finest
flowering of Mankind. You are the fount
of our wisdom, you are the source of our
strength, you are our Bastion against
Eunarchy. You are our hope, guide and
example for the next three thousand years.
Dynamic Erection is the Future!
Malcolm Scrawdyke is Dynamic Erection!
Malcolm Scrawdyke is the Future!
(*Switches tape on. Loud chanting—Hail
Scrawdyke, Hail Scrawdyke, Hail
Scrawdyke—recorded over and over again
by the four to produce the effect of a vast
number.* SCRAWDYKE *waits, then gives a
small wave meaning silence.* WICK *turns
knob. Chanting is faded out.*)

SCRAWDYKE: Friends. Fellow fighters. People of the
Nation.
Two years ago I awoke from the troubled
sleep of apathy. There was borne upon me
a dreadful feeling that something was
wrong with the state of our country.
Seeking the cause of this dismal intuition, I
look around me. On every side I saw
decadence, cynicism, apathy and decay.
For seventeen months, try as I might, by
night or by day, I could not rid myself of
the spectre that haunted me. In bed, on the
street, at work and at play it was always
before me. The spectre of a dying culture,
materially fat but completely lacking in any

of the spiritual direction, promise and aspiration which made our race great over the millennia.

At first, I was bewildered, I was completely unable to grasp the situation. How can this be? I asked myself. How could it happen? Where are the leaders, mentors, and poets who throughout History have been the guardians against such catastrophe? I sought the giants who would carry me on their broad backs out of the darkness. I sought in vain. Such mythical creatures are nowhere to be found. They no longer exist. We must become the giants ourselves!

(*Roar of approval from tape recorder. As it fades* SCRAWDYKE *continues.*)

Hemmed in on every side, pressed to our last gasp by the massed hordes of militant Eunarchy, those who are castrated themselves and whose sole aim is to castrate us to their level, surrounded by these eunuchs I realized that we the oppressed must take matters into our own hands. We must rally our forces and seize the initiative.

(*Another roar. As it subsides—*)

I am fighting for a new clean day, when young people can stand upright in dignity, when no one need be afraid of their next thought, when frankness and honesty are universally respected, when power in the State is drawn from virtue. I call upon you all to follow the Party of Dynamic Erection which has already so decisively lit a blazing beacon here in Huddersfield that makes men shield their eyes across the continents

(*Roar grows towards end of speech.*)
I say join us now and sweep to the power
which is your birthright. Once and for all
time let us obliterate the scum from the
face of the earth. Give me your present
and I will give you the Future. I am
Scrawdyke and I am here! I promise, I
pledge, I promise, I will, I offer you one
thing and one thing alone, I offer you
Dignity!
(*Sustained roar. After a while it changes to
the chant: Hail Scrawdyke, Hail Scrawdyke,
Hail Scrawdyke, Hail Scrawdyke—*
SCRAWDYKE *steps down from the table.*)

WICK: The crowd's surgin' round y'.
SCRAWDYKE: Yeh. They're frenzied with approval.
(*He nods and acknowledges crowd.*)
WICK: Come on Irwin it's your duty t' protect
the Leader.
INGHAM: Eh?
WICK: Keep close to 'im.
NIPPLE: Look out the's an assassin.
SCRAWDYKE: Where?
NIPPLE: 'Ere.
WICK: O.K. y're comin' at 'im.
NIPPLE: 'E doesn't see me.
SCRAWDYKE: I do.
WICK: Y've got a knife.
NIPPLE: A gun.
SCRAWDYKE: Both!
NIPPLE: Ai'm goin' t' use—noe Ai won't tell y'.
WICK: Irwin, the ever-alert bodyguard spots 'im.
Not me Irwin. 'Im— Come on do y' stuff
man!
INGHAM: What?
WICK: 'Url y'self between the Leader an' 'is

82

assailant.

INGHAM: There isn't room.

SCRAWDYKE: Get back Nipple. Don't be so bloody impetuous.
(WICK *takes the banner and props it up at the back on the room so that it forms a background.*)

NIPPLE: Waah, Ai could 'ave killed y' five times by this——

WICK: Get back. Right. Now start again.

NIPPLE: Ai'm smilin' as if Ai'm goin' t' shake 'ands with the great man.

WICK: But Irwin isn't fooled! Go on.
(*Pushes* INGHAM *who falls awkwardly between* NIPPLE *and* SCRAWDYKE *and half-heartedly pushes at* NIPPLE.)

SCRAWDYKE: Go on Irwin tackle 'im.

NIPPLE: Noe, noe, y' don't manage——

WICK: Course 'e does, y're not suggestin' y' succeed are y'?

NIPPLE: Hee hee.

SCRAWDYKE: Aye that's a role you'd like i'n't it?

NIPPLE: Well, y' ought t' be grateful. 'Oo else'd go t' trouble t' kill yoo?

SCRAWDYKE: I 'ave many enemies. I 'ave the capacity to arouse deep antagonisms.

NIPPLE: Noe. Ai'd say in the main most people liked y'.

SCRAWDYKE: How ridiculous can y' get?

WICK: Come on get on wi' this attempted assassination. Irwin pushes you off an' grabs the knife.

NIPPLE: Noe, not yet, Ai—
(*He gives* INGHAM *a clumsy but powerful shove.* INGHAM *is annoyed.* INGHAM *rushes at* NIPPLE *with surprising ferocity. He pushes*

83

and pummels NIPPLE *for a moment until his sudden spurt of anger abates.*)

Ey give up. Ey stop. Noe. Ugh. That 'urt. Noe stop it——

(WICK *switches the tape recorder off.*)

SCRAWDYKE: O.K. lads that's it. Irwin y've successfully saved my life.

WICK: An' you're dead.

NIPPLE: Noe, noe, Ai've escaped.

WICK: 'Ow could y' possibly 'ave escaped? Irwin 'ad 'old of y'.

NIPPLE: Err, 'e took it too seriously but Ai——

INGHAM: A'm sorry like if A—, but——

NIPPLE: Noe, Ai mean 'e wouldn't 'ave 'ad a chance t' do all that if it was reel. Ai'd just fire at point blank range an' then in the confusion Ai'd just run——

WICK: You can't run.

NIPPLE: 'Course Ai c'n run.

WICK: All right, actions speak louder 'an words. Let's see y'!

NIPPLE: Waagh. Don't be——

WICK: Let's see y'.

NIPPLE: Waar—Ai can't in 'ere, it's too small.

(WICK *runs round the room very rapidly.*)

Aar well——

WICK: Your turn!

NIPPLE: Ai could if Ai——

WICK: It's all yours.

NIPPLE: Waar——

(*Pause.* NIPPLE *starts to lumber.*)

WICK: Aha. As A said y're dead.

BLACKOUT

84

SCENE 6

Lights up. Dark outside. SCRAWDYKE *is pacing about.*

SCRAWDYKE: —Monday morning. Monday morning
already. I've got to have another go at Ann
tonight. Oh it's got t' be better than last
Friday's 'eroic performance. Got down to
'er place, didn't even manage t' get
through t' garden gate. If I 'adn't bumped
into 'er as I scuttled away I wouldn't 'ave
even seen 'er. Told 'er all about the Party,
worked meself into a frenzy. And what did
she say? "Sounds difficult." That was it.
That was 'er reaction. That's the
tremendous impact I made! Now come on.
It's no use cryin' over spilled—Scrawdyke.
I've got to work this out. Now—well she
'as t' walk up Princess Street. That's 'er
quickest way t' trolley stop in front o' t'
Co-op. Suppose she comes— There's only
one other way she can get there, on Buxton
Road. Yes, I know, I can 'ide in that
tunnel by Whitfield's shop. One end looks
down on Princess Street t' other end comes
out on Buxton Road. So I'm in the tunnel.
(*He acts this out.*)
So I watch down— Then I run up t' t'
other end. I keep a constant watch. One
way—then t' other. I see 'er comin'—say up
Princess Street, that's most likely. I watch
'er walk up. She might see me! No, no, it's

85

dark. Lurk man lurk. Right I watch 'er.
She comes up past. Suppose she's got
somebody wi' 'er. Oh they'll leave 'er at t'
top. I run up t' other end an' I can see 'er
go t' t' stop. What if a trolley comes and
picks 'er up before I can get there? Oh
well, that can't be 'elped. It's unlikely,
unlikely, unlikely. So I see 'er—then I come
out. Walk on towards 'er casual, just
walkin', upright, dignified. An' when I get
by 'er, I just see 'er, by accident. What if I
falter? I won't. I see 'er—"Ah, hullo. Just
come up from Tech? I'm just on me way
back to the Studio. Been out for a bit of a
stroll y' know. Look why don't y' pop in
for a cup o' tea if y're not doin' anything.
You invited me down t' your place an' I'd
like t' return the compliment. It's not
exactly a pent'ouse but it 'as one or two
amusin' features."
Get 'er in 'ere. Sit 'er down. Fire. Tea.
Record. Then— Tell 'er. Yes. Explain. I
need 'er. I want 'er. I'm shy— Oh I c'n do
it. The right atmosphere. I'm a remarkable
man. She'll soon see that. Once she
understands, I'm away. The's not really
anything t' stop me. The 'ole thing's
organic. I shall triumph.
"I'm glad I bumped into you Ann because
there are one or two things I'd like to say
to you. To begin with I must make it clear
that I am afflicted by shyness. And like all
who suffer this affliction my behaviour is
often misconstrued. I——"

BLACKOUT

Scene 7

WICK: Monday, Scrawdyke the Fifth, Year One.

SCRAWDYKE: Only three days t' go before the Great Day begins.

WICK: The beginning of the New Era.

(INGHAM *comes in, carrying a bundled sleeping-bag under his arm.*)

'Ail Scrawdyke.

INGHAM: 'Ail Scrawdyke. A've brought me sleepin'-bag. Oooh it's cold.

WICK: Aye there are six-foot drifts up our way.

INGHAM: Listen, like, A've got summat t' tell y'.

SCRAWDYKE: What?

INGHAM: Well, A were just gettin' off t' trolley—they're still runnin' all right but they're a bit—well anyway A just got off y' know, where it stops just outside t' Pack'orse front——

SCRAWDYKE: Yeh, yeh.

INGHAM: Ay well, A just got off an' A bumped int' Eric Boocock——

SCRAWDYKE: I 'ope y' didn't damage 'im. I want 'im 'ole for 'is trial.

WICK: Yeh 'e's on our list.

INGHAM: Aye, well, anyway 'e's walkin' up, y' know on 'is way back t' Tech, so like A walked on Cross Church Street with 'im, well some o' t' way, A left 'im by Jacksons. Anyway, 'e sez, like, there was this meetin' this mornin' an' Allard told 'em about— It

appears like 'at Allard, this mornin' called
'em all in t' t' end room at eleven o'clock.
An' 'e tells 'em 'ow me an' John 'ave—
well, left like. 'Ow we'd—A mean this's the
way 'e put it—'ow we'd gone against 'im.
An' then, apparently, A mean so Eric said,
'e tells 'em like as 'ow we've all 'ad it
now—A mean from what—well, could be
called a careers—y' know. An' 'ow it's
a—it's a— Well that doesn't— Anyway
that's what 'er——

SCRAWDYKE: "An' 'ow it's" what?

INGHAM: Eh?

SCRAWDYKE: Y' started t' say summat then y'——

INGHAM: Oh well that was—er—A mean it wasn't
anything.

SCRAWDYKE: I'm orderin' y' t' tell me what it is.

INGHAM: Oh, well, it was something an' nothin'. Just
that, y' know, 'e just said 'e thought we
were both, t' some extent—very promisin'—
students—an' by leavin' we've spoilt—A
mean this's just what 'e thinks. That's all.
A mean the's nothing——
(*Pause. The information has made* WICK
thoughtful.)

SCRAWDYKE: Well lads y' can see what 'e's tryin' t' do. I
must say I'm surprised 'at even 'e'd stoop
t' such a feeble old trick.

INGHAM: What d' y'——?

SCRAWDYKE: It stands out a mile Irwin. Boocock wasn't
at your bus stop by accident. 'E was
planted there by Allard. 'E's just one of
Allard's agents. 'E was deliberately sent
there t' tell y' all this stuff about promisin'
students t' try and make y' discontented.
It's the oldest trick in the book.

88

Huh, 'ere I've been goin' on about not
underestimatin' 'im. That'd be impossible.
If this's the level on which 'is mind works—
It's goin' t' be such a pushover we shan't
even need t' be 'ere. It'll 'appen by itself.
We can all leave town. Go out in t' t'
fields an' make a snowman.
I'm disappointed, I was lookin' forward to
some ex'ilaratin' action. Now I can see our
only problem's goin' t' be stiflin' the yawns.
(*Pause.*)

WICK: Yeh, yeh——

SCRAWDYKE: With every hour I grow more confident.
With every minute our task seems easier. I
'ave no worries about Allard. If I 'ave any
worries at all, they concern quite a diff'rent
personage.

INGHAM: 'Oo?

SCRAWDYKE: Isn't it obvious? Nipple.

WICK: Y' mean 'e's not t' be trusted.

SCRAWDYKE: That's exactly what I mean.

WICK: 'E's plannin' to betray us.

SCRAWDYKE: I'm afraid so.

INGHAM: But what makes y' think that?

SCRAWDYKE: 'E's paranoid. 'E 'as all the usual
symptoms.

WICK: Aye.

INGHAM: 'Ow d' y' mean?

SCRAWDYKE: Paranoea, clinically defined, is a syndrome
comprising: delusions of grandeur,
persecution mania, inability to reciprocate
positive emotions, love, trust, etc.,
alienation from environment. All
contributing to, and forming a part of, a
general tendency to inhabit a world of
fantasy.

89

WICK: That's a perfect description of Nipple.

SCRAWDYKE: 'E's bound to betray us. It's a compulsion with 'im.

WICK: 'E'd betray us even if 'e didn't want to.

INGHAM: Then why did y'——?

SCRAWDYKE: Why did I bring 'im in? Good question Irwin. I brought 'im in so that we could 'ave some control over 'im. Better to 'ave 'im plottin' on the inside than from the outside.

WICK: That assassination business wasn't just a game to Nipple.

SCRAWDYKE: It certainly wasn't. It revealed 'is true feelings. But we shall get in first. We must anticipate the event. We must conceive the exact nature of Nipple's treachery before 'e's 'ad a chance to conceive it for 'imself.

WICK: Charge 'im with it before 'e's even thought of it.

SCRAWDYKE: Such is the nature of political foresight.

WICK: What 'as 'e done then?

SCRAWDYKE: 'E's certainly 'ad a secret meetin' with Allard.

WICK: Of course, where an' when?

SCRAWDYKE: After dark.

WICK: 'E sent a message to Allard.

SCRAWDYKE: 'E did.

WICK: 'E disguised 'imself as a crocodile an' unobtrusively made 'is way into the Art School where 'e lingered outside Allard's door. When Allard came out 'e bit 'im on the ankle and lower leg then swiftly made 'is getaway. When Allard came to examine the bite marks 'e discovered that they formed a message in cuneiform script.

SCRAWDYKE: God, 'e's a cunning bastard.

WICK: Unfortunately Nipple's spelling let 'im down an' Allard ended up treadin' water for three hours in the Public Baths at Cleck'eaton.

SCRAWDYKE: 'E phoned Allard.

WICK: An' where did they meet?

SCRAWDYKE: Er—I know. At the top of St. Paul's church tower!

WICK: Yeh. Haha. Nobody'd think of goin' up there.

SCRAWDYKE: Yeh. The's a little narrer ledge just at the base o' t' actual spire. Y' know it's just a little parapet thing about two feet wide.

INGHAM: Oh aye, we climbed up there last summer.

WICK: Aye when we were doin' Arts Ball decorations in t' church.

SCRAWDYKE: Y' go through a little door 'idden in t' foyer, at t' base o' t' tower.

WICK: Yeh. Yeh the's just room t' squeeze y' way up them stairs an' they're so bloody steep. The's no light an' it's all coated wi' pigeon muck.

SCRAWDYKE: The perfect settin'. Especially in this weather.

INGHAM: Oo I wou'n't like to 'ave t' go up there in this weather.

SCRAWDYKE: It's just the place. It combines idiocy with infamy.

WICK: Yeh. When did they meet there.

SCRAWDYKE: Oh let's say they met there t'night. In a few hours' time. At 6.17.

WICK: Right. Let's make a tower.
(WICK *starts piling chairs and boxes on top of the table to form a spire.* SCRAWDYKE *helps him. They chuckle.* INGHAM *is amused too.*)

91

SCRAWDYKE: Good.
WICK: We've got just the—
(He goes to the tape recorder and runs it until he gets loud howling wind.)
Remember this?
SCRAWDYKE: Oh yeh. We used it for that——
INGHAM: Oh that.
WICK: Aye A never wiped it off.
SCRAWDYKE: Great. Now Nipple goes t' t' church first, 'e goes through that little door an' 'e starts t' grope up that spiral staircase.
(SCRAWDYKE, as NIPPLE, starts climbing round and round and round on the same spot, laboriously, and ever more wearily.)
'E's forgotten t' bring a torch.
(Lights match and peering myopically continues. Match goes out. He gropes constrictedly.)
WICK: Allard arrives ten minutes later an' starts.
(WICK starts spiralling.)
'E 'asn't got a torch either. Too cautious. Doesn't want t' be seen.
SCRAWDYKE: A pigeon craps on Nipple's 'ead. Daargh! Finally 'e nears the top.
(He drags himself the last few steps, each one a tremendous effort, the last step being on to the table by means of a chair. On the ledge he presses himself against the spire.)
It's freezin'. T' snow's teemin' down. It's pitch dark. T' wind nearly pulls 'im off t' ledge.
WICK: God A'm getting dizzy.
(SCRAWDYKE is edging his way round the spire.)
Allard reaches the summit.
(WICK gets on to the table and starts edging

round the spire in the opposite direction to
SCRAWDYKE. *Moving crab-wise pressed flat*
against the spire they draw nearer and
nearer to one another, until they bump,
pressed shoulder to shoulder.)
It is said that the rain in Spain falls mainly
on the plain.

SCRAWDYKE: Noe y've got it wrong. The's noe, "It is
said", yoo've put that in. Y' should 'ave
just said, "The rain in Spain falls mainly
on the plain."

WICK: That is outside my terms of reference. I
take it that you are the person with whom
I have an appointment.

SCRAWDYKE: Don't bee precipitate. Ai've got t' say mai
part first.

WICK: I realize that there is a certain protocol in
these matters but I urge you to make haste.

SCRAWDYKE: Say yours again.

WICK: Oh very well, if you insist. The rain in
Spain falls mainly on the plain.

SCRAWDYKE: Except in July when none falls from the
sky. Yoo're late!

WICK: I apologize.

SCRAWDYKE: Keep movin'. It's less suspicious.
(*They edge precariously round, frozen and*
unable to see, in danger of being torn from
the ledge by the wind.)

WICK: I believe you have something to tell me.

SCRAWDYKE: Scrawdyke is goin' to kidnap yoo on
Friday night.

WICK: What time?

SCRAWDYKE: Nine o'clock.

WICK: Good God! Are you certain of the validity
of this statement?

SCRAWDYKE: Certain.

WICK: Then on the basis of this information I shall undertake certain measures.

SCRAWDYKE: What about mai reward?

WICK: I will ensure that you get the scholarship to study in Tahiti. You're sure no one knows of this meeting?

(SCRAWDYKE *stops.* WICK *goes on moving.*)

Where are you?

SCRAWDYKE: Ai'm 'ere. Where are yoo?

WICK: I'm here. Where have you gone?

SCRAWDYKE: Ai'm here.

WICK: Where?

SCRAWDYKE: 'Ere.

WICK: The other side?

SCRAWDYKE: Come to mee.

WICK: No you come to me.

SCRAWDYKE: Noe, noe, yoo come to mee.

WICK: No, no, you come to me.

SCRAWDYKE: Noe you come to mee.

WICK: All right stay where you are.

SCRAWDYKE: Which way are yoo comin'?

WICK: I don't know. I've lost all sense of direction.

(WICK *gropes round, and not seeing* SCRAWDYKE *is on top of him before he realizes it. They are squeezed on top of each other.*)

Aah!

SCRAWDYKE: Get away. Get away.

WICK: You move out of the way.

SCRAWDYKE: Noe yoo move out of the way.

WICK: Let me pass.

SCRAWDYKE: Noe let me pass.

WICK: Let me——

SCRAWDYKE: ⎫ Let mee, let mee
WICK: ⎭ Let me, let me—

94

(*They struggle, entangled together.*)

WICK: I am the Principal of a School of Art.

SCRAWDYKE: Ai am a great novelist.

(*They fall off—*)

WICK:
SCRAWDYKE: } Aaaaaaaaaaaaaaaaa—

(*—on to the floor where they roll about laughing then dog-hooting.* SCRAWDYKE *sits up.*)

SCRAWDYKE: Well Irwin I 'ope you took note of all that because you are the witness.

INGHAM: Witness?

WICK: Yes man. You saw it all.

INGHAM: Well where am I supposed to 'ave been?

WICK: Sittin' on the lightning conductor.

SCRAWDYKE: Where were you Irwin at approximately 6.17 this evening?

INGHAM: On top o' St. Paul's Church tower.

BLACKOUT

SCENE 8

SCRAWDYKE *comes in. Remains in the dark.*

SCRAWDYKE: Go back! Go back! Go back! No I— Oh I
walked straight past. Straight past—I just
couldn't make— Straight on. Did she see
me? Oh I don't know. Didn't even dare
look at 'er. Oh!— Go back now before—
No, no. Oh let's face it! Let's face it this's
the end of any— I've shown meself just
now—completely spineless. I'm the most
feeble. Ough! It makes me so— I want t'—
Do something! Get! Hurt! Nipple! I'll get
that bastard tomorrow. I've got t' get my—
I'll show 'im! This's a bill that 'e can pay!

SCENE 9

Lights up. Afternoon light is fading. SCRAWDYKE, WICK *and* INGHAM *are sitting about.* NIPPLE'S *tread on the stairs. They all watch door.* NIPPLE *enters.* SCRAWDYKE *points at him.*

NIPPLE: What are yoo pointin' that finger at?

SCRAWDYKE: Traitor!

NIPPLE: Eh?

SCRAWDYKE: Tergiversator!

(WICK *gets up, gestures to* INGHAM *and they start removing the boxes from the table and arranging the room for a trial.* SCRAWDYKE'S *chair behind table, chairs for witness and prosecutor, tea-chest for prisoner, banner propped up behind* SCRAWDYKE'S *chair.*)

WICK: O.K. Nipple the game's up. The cat's out of the bag, the beans 'ave been spilled.

NIPPLE: Err— Another of your elaborate jokes Ai suppose.

SCRAWDYKE: It's no joke.

WICK: I've never 'eard of anything so unfunny.

NIPPLE: What the 'eck are y' talkin' about?

SCRAWDYKE: I have just received incontestable proof that at 6.17 yesterday evening you met and conspired with Philip Allard, Arch Eunuch, and Enemy of the Party, at the top of St. Paul's Church tower with the purpose of betraying the Dynamic Erectionist Movement.

97

NIPPLE: Hee hee. Now A know y're not serious. St. Paul's Church tower, hee hee.

WICK: That's a laugh that'll rapidly commute across your face my friend. Ev'rything's ready.

(SCRAWDYKE *sits in his chair.* INGHAM *sits to one side.*)

You stand in there.

(*Indicates tea-chest.*)

NIPPLE: Why?

SCRAWDYKE: Come on stand in there.

NIPPLE: Oh Ai suppose Ai've got t' 'umour y'.

(WICK *sits down near the opposite end of the table from* INGHAM.)

SCRAWDYKE: Minister Blagden. As Minister of Justice and Prosecutor-General you will undertake the prosecution.

WICK: Zealously my leader.

SCRAWDYKE: You will also place yourself at the disposal of the Prisoner should the Tribunal deem it necessary.

WICK: Y' see Nipple, ev'rything's fair and square. Y've got a Defence Counsel.

NIPPLE: Y' can't 'ave the same man both prosecuting and defendin'. It's un'eard of.

WICK: Oh no it isn't. Y've just 'eard of it.

NIPPLE: Waarh. It wouldn't be allowed in a proper court.

SCRAWDYKE: We're not int'rested in British legal procedure. This tribunal is constituted according to Dynamic Erectionist procedure.

NIPPLE: What's that?

WICK: You'll find out.

(SCRAWDYKE *stands.*)

SCRAWDYKE: The Tribunal will rise.

98

NIPPLE: Hee hee.

SCRAWDYKE: On behalf of the Dynamic Erectionist
Party, I hereby declare this Special Tribunal
convened on the Sixth Day of Scrawdyke,
Year One, in secret session, for the
investigation of crimes against the Party,
duly and legitimately open.

WICK: Hail Scrawdyke!

SCRAWDYKE: ⎱
INGHAM: ⎰ Hail Scrawdyke!

NIPPLE: Hee hee.

SCRAWDYKE: Dennis Charles Nipple, I charge you with
Treason against the Party, entering into a
Conspiracy with the Arch Enemy of the
Party, Philip Allard, betraying your oath
of allegiance, and generally being in league
with the Forces of World Eunarchy.
(SCRAWDYKE, INGHAM *and* NIPPLE *sit*.)

NIPPLE: Ai must 'ave been very busy to 'ave done
all that.

WICK: 'Ow d' you plead? Guilty or Very Guilty?

NIPPLE: Ai plead Not Guilty.

WICK: There's no such plea.

NIPPLE: That's ridiculous. Y' can't say Ai'm guilty
before Ai've been tried.

WICK: We can and do. This's a Dynamic
Erectionist Tribunal. Y' can either plead
Guilty or Very Guilty. You 'ave that
choice.

NIPPLE: That's noe choice.

WICK: It is. And not only that it's your
inalienable right.

NIPPLE: Err, it's not fair.

SCRAWDYKE: It's not the business of this Tribunal to be
fair. Fairness doesn't enter into it. We're
here to investigate the depth and scope of

99

your crimes not whether they 'appened.

WICK: It doesn't matter to us whether or not they did 'appen. The possibility that they might 'ave 'appened is sufficient. Even if you could prove conclusively that they did not, in fact, take place it wouldn't make any difference.

SCRAWDYKE: I must say that it's my personal opinion that they didn't. But it's quite irrelevant.

NIPPLE: Then 'ow——

WICK: The fact that we can conceive of them 'appenin' is sufficient.

SCRAWDYKE: The existence of this Tribunal is your indictment.

NIPPLE: Well in that case if Ai c'n conceive 'at you're capable of some crime it means you're guilty too.

SCRAWDYKE: Certainly not.

NIPPLE: Why?

SCRAWDYKE: Because we're trying you. You're not trying us.

WICK: Because we're calling the tune and you aren't. That gives us the right to be right.

NIPPLE: Hee hee, if this wasn't a joke it'd be a surreal nightmare.

WICK: The prisoner refused to take his case seriously and spoke flippantly.

NIPPLE: Hee hee.

WICK: Well 'ow d' y' plead?

NIPPLE: Ai don't plead at all. Ai don't recognize this tribunal or whatever y' like t' call it.

WICK: So y're pullin' the old Charles the First bit on us.

NIPPLE: What d' y' mean?

SCRAWDYKE: If 'e wants t' play at Charles the First let 'im. It's fairly well known 'ow Charles the

100

First ended up.

NIPPLE: Y've got the wrong king.

WICK: Y' what?

NIPPLE: It wasn't Charles the First it was Charles the Second.

WICK: We'll just add that t' the list of charges. Distortin' 'istory for 'is own ends.

SCRAWDYKE: 'E pleads Very Guilty.

NIPPLE: Ai don't plead anything.

WICK: That is construed as pleadin' Very Guilty.

SCRAWDYKE: It is.

WICK: I think in a case like this, a case as serious as this, an exceptional plea of Very Very Guilty should be allowed.

SCRAWDYKE: The Tribunal grants your request.

NIPPLE: Well if Ai'm so guilty, what's the point in tryin' me?

WICK: We can't just let you get away with any old claim. You may be over-statin' y'r case. You may not be anywhere as guilty as you plead. We've got t' see whether you're coal black or charcoal grey. The safety and future of the Party depend on it.

SCRAWDYKE: Minister of Propaganda, Justice and the Interior, Prosecutor-General, I call upon you to open the case for the prosecution.

WICK: I call upon the witness, Irwin Ingham, to lay his deposition before the tribunal.

INGHAM: Eh?

WICK: Witness Ingham, will you please tell us exactly what you saw and heard yesterday evening.

INGHAM: Oh—well—er—what um——

WICK: Far be it from me to put words into your mouth. Just tell the Tribunal in your own words what you saw and heard.

101

INGHAM: Oh—aye—well— Well—I er—A mean they
were up—an' um, an' 'e said er—what it
was like, an' y' see I'd been walkin', A
mean A was walkin', just by there, an' as
A was walkin' A saw like 'em, y' know,
like goin' in, like goin' into it. Well I didn't
know—A mean I didn't know—then, y'
know, er— Well, A mean, A wondered.
So, like, as A say, they went—A mean they
went in, an' then, well, A suppose they
went up. Well one at a time—like—A mean
that's what— And anyway, as A say, one
went up, one of 'em, then—then the other
like and er— And anyway when they'd—
when they'd gone up, gone in, y' know, an'
they'd well, they'd got there, got up there,
to the top of—y' know, where it er—was—
Well—they met A suppose. A mean like
they did like— Then, then when they
were—this—well they er—A mean they
er—to each. A mean when they went in,
when they first went in, when one went in
an' then the other, 'e went in, well then I
went, I went in, y' know because it just
seemed a bit— Anyway, so, as A say, I
went—I followed, A suppose y' might say,
that, an' A saw 'em go, through this—an'
then go up—an' I—an' when I, A mean
when I got—they were er—y' know. An'
when they'd finished well, they came, they
came down. They came down an' went
out, an' then I came down an' I went out.
A mean after they'd come down, come out,
gone down, come out, I'd gone, A mean
come, A mean out—I'd, well, y' know—
An' so really that's er—what I c'n, y' know,

102

that's just er—that is what, well, y' know—
that's it.

WICK: Thank you. So there you are. Conclusive
testimony on the part of an eyewitness.

NIPPLE: Waah. 'E didn't——

SCRAWDYKE: Silence! The prisoner is not permitted to
speak at this juncture.

WICK: So there we 'ave it in all its disgustin'
detail. You were seen entering St. Paul's
Church, climbing the tower, and up·there
on the ledge, you were overheard
conspiring with the Arch Eunuch, and
Enemy of the Party, Philip Allard, whom
you had previously arranged to meet there
by phone. You informed him of all the
Party's secret plans in return for a glossy
picture-book of Tahitian nudes and your
picture in the 'Uddersfield Daily Examiner.
I submit that the case is fully proved
against the Enemy of the Party, Dennis
Charles Nipple.

SCRAWDYKE: I now call upon the Minister of Justice and
Prosecutor-General to open the case for
the defence.

NIPPLE: Ai'll conduct mai own defence.

SCRAWDYKE: That can't be allowed. You'll be allowed
an opportunity to speak at the proper time.

NIPPLE: Waargh.

WICK: The defence rests.

NIPPLE: Waargh.

SCRAWDYKE: The prisoner will now be allowed to
confess.

NIPPLE: What d' y' mean confess? Hee hee. Ai
didn't even know y' could get up that
church tower.

WICK: Ignorance is no excuse.

NIPPLE: Well Ai suppose y' must 'ave y' little games.

SCRAWDYKE: I don't play games Nipple. I never 'ave an' I never will. I've never played a game in my life. I hate games. I've always avoided 'em. I'll show you whether I'm playin' games.

(*He rises.*)

WICK: The Tribunal will rise.

(INGHAM *and* NIPPLE *get up.*)

NIPPLE: Waah.

SCRAWDYKE: It is the sentence of this Tribunal that Dennis Charles Nipple shall firstly be expelled from the Party of Dynamic Erection. And that secondly he is sentenced to death. The execution of the second part of this sentence not being practical in the present circumstances is suspended until such time as it is practicable whereupon it will be carried out summarily. It is my Decree as Leader of the Dynamic Erectionist Party, that until such time as the sentence can be executed, Dennis Charles Nipple shall be totally ostracized by all the members of the Party, that his name must not even be mentioned and that he be regarded as having ceased to exist except for the purpose of carrying out the Sentence of Death.

(NIPPLE *looks round at the set faces.*)

NIPPLE: But——

WICK: Y're dead Nipple. For all intents an' purposes y're now a corpse.

NIPPLE: But y' must be—A mean y' can't really— Ai mean it's—Ai mean if y' really do, did— It'd mean— It'd mean y' were mad.

SCRAWDYKE: I'm mad! I'm mad! Y' 'eard what 'e said,
I'm mad! 'E sez I'm mad! That's really
convincin' coming from you. It really rings
true. The phantom novelist, the solipsist,
the egoist, the surrealist figment of y're
own diseased imagination! The fantast 'oo
c'n quite seriously arrange t' meet the
'eadmaster of an Art School on an icy
ledge on the top of rickety church tower in
a blizzard in the middle of winter—'e says
I'm mad! Y' just couldn't wait. Y' always
'ave t' be the centre. Y' can't submit y're
own perverted ego t' something bigger than
y'self. You've betrayed me! Me personally!
I brought you in. I trusted you. I gave you
ev'rything. I give. I open, I trust, and you
defecate on me as soon as— Well you'll
find I have another side. I'll show you. I'll
get you. You degenerate imbecile! I shan't
forget. The day'll come. I'll hunt you down
to the ends of the earth. I'll follow. I'll
track. I'll make you wish you'd never been
born. I could strangle you with my bare
hands! I could drive a six-inch nail through
your head! I've been too quick for you. I
always am. I'm always in front. I always
am. I always will be. I'll get you. I'll get
you. I will, I'll show, I'll——
(*He is shaking and speechless with rage. The
other three are transfixed. Pause.*)
NIPPLE: Y' mean it.
(*Pause.*)
But—why?
SCRAWDYKE: Why? Because I!
NIPPLE: Ai—Ai don't know why y' should want t'
do this t' mee. Ai never did—an' y' know

105

that, y' said that. Ai mean Ai can't see why
it is y'—Ai've always 'ad—Ai've always
resp—Ai've always 'ad an 'igh respect for
you. Ai know we've 'ad our disagreements
an' Ai've disagreed but—Ai can't see why
y' want t' do this t' mee. Why should y'?
Ai mean Ai've always thought you were a
man, one man in this town 'oo was above,
essentially above mere petty spite. Ai might
not 'ave told y', 'ave said it to y', but then
it's not mai nature. Ai don't find it easy. Is
that what y' want? Y' want to see me
grovel? Well if it is Ai'm not goin' t' say
Ai'm not 'urt by what y've just said. Ai
thought you were the only one 'oo—Ai
valued our friendship. An' now y' want t'
do this.—Oh come on Mal, let me in on it,
Ai know it's not a game, but tell me it's a
re'earsal for some trial yoo intend to 'old
in the future for some reel enemy of the
party.

SCRAWDYKE: It was your trial.

NIPPLE: Y' really want me t' go? An' if y' could
y'd really 'ave me killed?

SCRAWDYKE: Yes!

NIPPLE: Well—that's bad. That's really very bad.
All these years and Ai thought you were
mai friend. It's bad for mee but it's even
worse for you. Ai feel sorry for y'.

SCRAWDYKE: Get out of my sight!

NIPPLE: All right.

WICK: And if you dare to say a word or write a
word——

NIPPLE: Don't worry! Ai've no desire t' write about
you or anything t' do wi' y'. It's beneath
me, unworthy of mee!

106

(He shuffles to the door and opens it.)
Ai go an' we shall never meet again. But
Ai want y' to know that whyever and
'owever you've persecuted mee—Ai forgive
you.
*(He goes out, closes the door. His slow tread
is heard going down the stairs. The
remaining three stand motionless.)*

BLACKOUT

Scene 10

Lights up. INGHAM'S *sleeping-bag is stretched out on the floor.* INGHAM *is lighting the gas-ring. During the following he puts kettle on and makes tea.* WICK *comes in.*

WICK: 'Ail Scrawdyke!

INGHAM: Oh aye. 'E's not 'ere.

WICK: Where is 'e?

INGHAM: 'E's gone for a prowl round.

WICK: Oh.

INGHAM: 'E likes that, prowlin' around.

WICK: Aye. 'Ow d' y' kip?

INGHAM: Well A mean——

WICK: Yeh.

INGHAM: A'm just mekkin' some tea.

WICK: Great. There are six-foot drifts up our way.

INGHAM: Up Cowcliffe.

WICK: Yeh. Ey listen. Me ma rang up Allard this mornin'.

INGHAM: Eh!

WICK: Yeh. She wanted t' know why me grant 'adn't come through. Y' know they usually send t' cheque about t' second day o' term. I tried t' bluff 'er, y' know, sayin' it'd just been 'eld up or summat. But it didn't work an' this mornin' she phoned 'im.

INGHAM: Oh. What 'appened?

WICK: Oh t' 'ole bloody thing came out. Now she knows why I 'avn't been goin' int' Tech ev'ry mornin', she knows A'm not just preparin' me thesis at 'ome. Man she went spare, she gave me the full treatment, either beg Allard t' tek me back or never darken 'er doorstep again.

INGHAM: Oh just t' same as me mam.

WICK: Aye.

INGHAM: Y' goin' t' move in 'ere then?

WICK: Well——

INGHAM: Oh—it's the 7th now. Two days t' go——

WICK: Listen Irwin, y' know the plan for Friday, 'ow feasible d' y' think it is?

INGHAM: Well——

WICK: Just between you an' me.

INGHAM: What just——

WICK: Yeh, without—just between you an' me.

INGHAM: Well—A think there are, is, A mean it does present—certain difficulties.

WICK: Exactly.

INGHAM: But it doesn't—A mean like the's nowt we c'n——

WICK: There is. I 'avn't told y' what Allard said t' me mother. 'E said 'at if you an' me apologize to 'im 'e'd consider tekkin' us back an' gettin' us grants goin' again. But 'e said we 'ad t' do it tomorra, Thursday, or it's no go.

INGHAM: But we——

WICK: Look, I don't like the idea of crawlin' back t' that bastard any more 'an you do.

INGHAM: A wasn't thinkin' of 'im.

WICK: Aye. Well. Don't worry about that. I'm not suggestin' we walk out on Mal, desert the party, 'course not. I still want it t' succeed as much as I ever did. I'm goin' t' suggest a change of tactics that's all.

INGHAM: Oh 'e'll never——

WICK: It's for the good of the Party man. This thing on Friday's too much of a one-shot risk.

INGHAM: It's tekken y' a long time t' see that.

WICK: Well we all got carried away. Now's the time for realistic reappraisal.

INGHAM: Try tellin' Mal that.

WICK: Y're too much afraid of 'im. I'll persuade 'im.

INGHAM: 'Oo'es ever managed t' persuade Malcolm Scrawdyke except Malcolm Scrawdyke.

WICK: Don't worry we've got a good case, I'll put it to 'im. Don't worry, 'e'll see it, don't worry.

INGHAM: Well A wish A could be so——

WICK: Don't worry Irwin. Let's 'ave some o' this witch piss.
(*Pours tea.*)
We've only missed a week down there.
Less 'an that.
(*Looking at* SCRAWDYKE'S *self-portrait.*)
Mal's not a painter.

INGHAM: I'd just started a litho, some fish, but they'll 'ave gone off by now.

WICK: Be nice t' do some paintin' again.

INGHAM: Aye. A suppose A could get some more.

WICK: Y' know, for N.D.D., they provide y' wi' new canvases.

INGHAM: Aye A know they——

WICK: Nice virgin springy new canvases. It's a great feelin' when y' put y' brush on to a new canvas an' y' feel that life in it. Sends a ripple up y'r arm man.
(*Footsteps.*)

INGHAM: Oh A'm not lookin' forward t' this.

WICK: Don't get flustered just be natural.

INGHAM: Well A—oh——
  (SCRAWDYKE *comes in.*)
WICK: Hail Scrawdyke!
SCRAWDYKE: 'Ail Scrawdyke. Give us some o' that tea.
INGHAM: Oh yeh.
SCRAWDYKE: No milk?
INGHAM: No.
SCRAWDYKE: Ah! The's nowt like a cup o' tea! I've just been down t' St. Paul's Street t' look over the snow situation.
WICK: Oh yeh, very important. It's not too thick down there is it?
SCRAWDYKE: Nah it's not too thick. I made my way down there, I moved cautiously. I took great care not t' be seen. Allard 'as spies ev'rywhere, anybody might be an Allard spy. But I know 'ow t' slink through this town without bein' seen. All the loose stuff's been cleared off St. Paul's, they've got cinders down. The rest o' the route's clear too. T' snow's there but it's been pressed down smooth an' tight. As I walked along the route I saw the irony, I saw us glidin' 'ere on Friday night over the Royal road they're keepin' clear to their own destruction.
WICK: Oh well that's um— Listen Mal, me an' Irwin 'ave been, well, lookin' at certain aspects of the plan from a few new angles.
SCRAWDYKE: Well there's nothing I like better than a new angle.
WICK: Yeh I know that. That's why——
SCRAWDYKE: I'm always open to new ideas. Some men can't keep out germs or damp, I can't keep out new ideas.
WICK: Sure I know that. That's why these new

111

ideas are goin' t' make our success even more certain than it is now.

(SCRAWDYKE *sits in his chair*.)

SCRAWDYKE: The day I can no longer take in a new idea is the day I shall climb down the nearest grate an' allow myself to be sluiced away with all the other refuse.

WICK: An' I'll be there, with y'. We'll get flushed down t' Bradley Sewerage Works t'gether. We c'n compare notes an' share the sights. But, anyway listen——

SCRAWDYKE: Fire away.

WICK: Right. Well listen Mal, I've been thinkin' about the plan for Friday, Scrawdyke the Ninth. Now first of all A want t' say, y' know, I still think it's a great idea. It's more than that, it's a magnificent idea, it's a stroke of genius. There can be no two ways about that, it's a magnificent idea, it's a great plan. An' A'm not knockin' it, get that clear, I'm not for a minute knockin' it. I'd never knock it. It could achieve ev'rything we want, it could do it in one stroke, A mean that's t' 'ole beauty o' it. But, an' I only say this after a great deal of thought, y' know, after lookin' at the 'ole question thoroughly, which as realistic revolutionaries we must do, A mean that's what you've always said and I'm the first to agree. A mean be clear about this, I'm with you over the Party and our aims up to the 'ilt. Don't think A'm wavering, not a bit. What A'm goin' t' suggest is only becos I'm committed, y' know, one hundred per cent, to the movement. An' what I say is only prompted by the desire

112

that we should succeed an' by nothin' else.
Now what A'm tryin' t' say is, there's only
one thing wrong with the plan as it stands
at the moment, not the actual plan itself,
as I say if it worked out it'd be
magnificent. No I'm not criticizin' it as a
plan, I'm only sayin' that there's a risk,
well perhaps not even that, but let's say a
possibility that it could fail. Not through
any blunder on our part, A mean that's
inconceivable, but through some factor
completely outside our control. Now I'm
not afraid for personal reasons, neither is
Irwin, we've put our all into this Party an'
if necessary we'd lay down our lives for it.
That's the ultimate sacrifice any
conspirator accepts from the word go an'
we don't shirk it. Whatever risks there are
we're right at your side, ready t' take
whatever comes. A mean let's not beat
about the bush, y're a great man, a great
Leader, and nobody appreciates that more
than I do. An' it's becos of all this that I
don't think we should stake ev'rything on
one throw. It'd be a tragedy, a cataclysmic
tragedy, if we were t' stake the future of
the Party, the future of the country even
the future of the world, on one act,
'owever great, an' it misfired through no
fault of ours. It's all a matter of timin'. It
could be another Beer 'All Putsch of 1923.
That put 'Itler back ten years. 'E tried too
much too soon. We can learn from that
mistake. We're more on the ball. So listen
'ere's the new idea. We play it really cool,
really really cool. Irwin and I go down to

113

Allard t'morra an' beg 'im t' take us back.
We really lay it on for 'im so 'e thinks
we're completely 'umiliated. Haha, y'
know, we feed 'im all that crap about
wantin' t' do finals, realizin' we'd
jeopardized our careers, 'at we've realized
we 'ave responsibilities, t' parents, teachers,
talent, society, the 'ole shit'ouse. "I think
we've grown up a little in the past few
days, sir."
We'll make tears run down 'is face. We'll
completely fool 'im. But the important
thing is we'll be back inside, we'll be able
t' strike at 'im from the inside. An' get
this, y'll love this, we'll tell 'im we saw
through you. We'll say we've realized
you're a complete shit. 'At you just tried to
get some lolly out of us an' when y' found
out we were skint y' ran out on us. But
then, an' this's the clincher, we'll say y're
'armless. Allard'll relax, 'e'll withdraw 'is
spies, 'e'll think it's all over, ev'rything's
cosy in 'is neat little world again. But we'll
be down there an' you'll be up 'ere. All the
time we seem t' be quietly working, we'll
be watchin'. Ev'ry night you'll 'ave a
detailed report on all 'is movements. We'll
be able t' find out 'is movements months
ahead. On any given day. An' all the time
we can build up our numbers, a few more
members of the right calibre could make
things easier. We could get cells started up
all over, Bradford, Leeds, 'Alifax,
Brig'ouse, Batley, even further afield, so 'at
when the moment arrived they'd be ready
t' sound the call in all those towns. We'd be

114

in a far better position than we are now. All the time you'd be up 'ere drawin' the noose ever tighter. Just think what a great sense of 'idden power that'd give y'. With Allard off the alert y' could move about quite freely. We'd put it round y'd settled down to a quite normal existence. Ha we could even say y'd got married. An' all the time we'd be preparing, drawin' the noose tighter, with no risks 'owever remote. Then suddenly, out of this calm will suddenly erect the penis of our conspiracy! Well Mal, what d' y' think? Eh, what d' y' think?—Come on Mal, what d' y' think of it?—It's a great plan. Now y've 'eard it, what d' y' reckon? Come on Mal, what d' y' think? (*Pause.*)

SCRAWDYKE: Phht!

BLACKOUT

SCENE 11

Lights up. Mid-afternoon. WICK *sits dejectedly, a blanket round him.* INGHAM *has his sleeping-bag round his legs.* SCRAWDYKE *is standing looking out of the window.*

SCRAWDYKE: Scrawdyke the Ninth. Not long to go before zero hour. The Old Era is drawing towards its close.

WICK: Oooo it's cold!

INGHAM: Seems t' get colder.

WICK: A'm sure it's never been as cold as this before.

INGHAM: Aye. I'n't it time we 'ad this fire on again?

SCRAWDYKE: No.

INGHAM: It's nearly three.

SCRAWDYKE: Not until quarter past.

WICK: T' last time we 'ad it on was one o'clock.

SCRAWDYKE: Quarter of an hour every two hours.

WICK: 'Ow d' y' get quarter past three then?

SCRAWDYKE: We count from the last switchin' off.

WICK: Switchin' on.

SCRAWDYKE: Switchin' off.

INGHAM: Switchin' on.

SCRAWDYKE: Switchin' off.

WICK: When we 'ad it on at one——

SCRAWDYKE: Quarter past, I——

INGHAM: No A think John's——

WICK: Y' switched it on y'self at one, A remember, y' asked Irwin.

INGHAM: Aye that's——

116

SCRAWDYKE: Well if what y' say—an' I don't—it was an oversight.

WICK: Oh hell what's quarter of an——

SCRAWDYKE: It's a matter of policy, a matter of plannin'. That shillin's got t' be conserved.

INGHAM: But now we're so near to—y' know— surely it doesn't like—A mean 'ow much money 'ave we?

WICK: You're the Minister of Finance.

INGHAM: But 'e's got the money.

SCRAWDYKE: As leader I ask for an' am allocated funds by you as Minister of Finance. I decide policy an' policy requires money. Your job is to keep account and find money.

INGHAM: Aye so it seems.

WICK: 'Ow much 'ave we got?

SCRAWDYKE: At this moment we 'ave two an' sixpence.

WICK: Well look why can't we 'ave another bob for the gas? It's so cold we're all stiff——

SCRAWDYKE: I never felt better, never felt——

WICK: Well Irwin an' me are stiff. We don't want to be stiff when the time comes, we want to be supple and ready for——

SCRAWDYKE: All right lads. I've decided t' make a policy change. You two go over t' t' Gates Café an' get a shilling. Spend the other one and six as y' see fit. Get another bob for the gas, get a couple o' teas, whatever y' fancy. I delegate the decision to you. I step completely out of the situation and leave it all t' you.

WICK: Right. Come on Irwin.

INGHAM: Aye.

SCRAWDYKE: But make sure y're back 'ere in good time for zero hour.

INGHAM: Aren't you comin'?

117

SCRAWDYKE: No.
WICK: Come on.
(*They go out.*)
SCRAWDYKE: Got rid of 'em for a while. Think a few
things out. Let's 'ave this bloody fire on. I
can 'ear 'em comin' up, turn it off. They'll
never be able t' work out 'ow much the'
was in it. An' if they do complain A'll tell
'em it's a faulty meter. Well it's been a
near scrape lately. Yeh, but I've managed.
I c'n keep 'em goin', but it's not goin' t'
be— Oh what's goin' t' 'appen tomorra?
It's all nonsense just one long wank, that's
all it is, from beginnin' to end. An' I'll
never dare try, not even try! I'm so weak,
no will, supine—I feel so ill, gnawin' in me
stomach, constipated— Oh! What else is
there now 'at Ann's—? I've got t' try, it
doesn't matter 'at it can't succeed, it only
matters 'at I lead— If only we do
something it doesn't matter. I've just got to
throw myself into it, do it without thought,
in a trance. Yes, that's it. A trance is
necessary for action. Just lead 'em through
that blasted door— Yes, yes— Ooogh!
(*He huddles by the fire. Crouching down to
it. The door opens quietly and* ANN GEDGE,
*in her early twenties, in an overcoat, a scarf
round her head, comes in. She stands just
inside the door.* SCRAWDYKE *doesn't notice
her.*)
Just act—act—that's it— Don't think—
Act, act, yes—that's—
(*He turns round and sees her.*)
Wah!
(*Jumps up. They stare at each other. Then*

118

ANN *closes the door and starts moving
slowly round the room examining its
contents; the sink full of filthy pots, the
painted boards, the rubbish, the dustbin, the
self-portrait, etc. Ending up looking at the
banner.* SCRAWDYKE *watches her transfixed.*)

ANN: So—this is it.

SCRAWDYKE: This is what?

ANN: 3a Commercial Chambers.

SCRAWDYKE: Oh.

(*Pause.*)

ANN: That's where y' sleep?

SCRAWDYKE: Yes.

ANN: Comfy?

SCRAWDYKE: All right.

ANN: Warm?

SCRAWDYKE: Enough.

ANN: Mm. 'Oos's the sleepin'-bag?

SCRAWDYKE: Irwin's.

ANN: 'E sleeps 'ere too?

SCRAWDYKE: Yes.

ANN: Y' all sleep 'ere?

SCRAWDYKE: Yes.

ANN: You eat up 'ere too?

SCRAWDYKE: Sometimes.

ANN: 'Oo cooks?

SCRAWDYKE: 'Ooever——

ANN: 'Ooever feels like it?

SCRAWDYKE: 'Ooever's allocated to it.

ANN: Oh. You don't do any.

SCRAWDYKE: I didn't say I didn't.

ANN: Y' do?

SCRAWDYKE: When the need arises.

ANN: What d' y' cook?

SCRAWDYKE: Well——

ANN: What d' y' make?

119

SCRAWDYKE: The usual things.

ANN: Such as.

SCRAWDYKE: Well, such as—just the usual——

ANN: Nothing fancy.

SCRAWDYKE: Certainly not.

ANN: Just good solid plain stuff?

SCRAWDYKE: Yes.

ANN: 'Oo's the best cook?

SCRAWDYKE: What?

ANN: 'Oo's the best cook?

SCRAWDYKE: Well—we're all more or less the same.

ANN: But you c'n 'old y'r own?

SCRAWDYKE: I c'n wield a pan.

ANN: When the need arises.

SCRAWDYKE: Yes.

ANN: An' y' cook on that?

SCRAWDYKE: Yes.

ANN: No stove.

SCRAWDYKE: No.

ANN: Where d' y' keep the utensils?

SCRAWDYKE: Oh—around.

ANN: Oh, y' keep 'em in the sink.
(*She lifts a battered filthy pan out of the sink.*)
Heinz Spaghetti. Burnt. 'Oo does the washin' up?

SCRAWDYKE: Nobody.

ANN: Y' still believe in fairies.

SCRAWDYKE: If we want a cup or a plate we just douse it off. We don't make a song and dance out of it.

ANN: A song an' a dance wi' a cup an' a plate. Sounds entertainin'.

SCRAWDYKE: Well we don't go in for it. I don't concern myself with things like that.

ANN: And this is the banner. Mm.

(*She sits in* SCRAWDYKE'S *chair. Pause.*)

SCRAWDYKE: Erm—erm—y're er— Y've just er—come from Tech?

ANN: Mm.

SCRAWDYKE: Oh— Y' didn't 'ave an evenin' class t'night?

(ANN *nods.*)

Oh—so you er—you er—decided to um—come away?

ANN: Huhuh.

SCRAWDYKE: An' you er—you er——

ANN: I came 'ere.

(*She gets out cigarettes, lights herself one.*)

'Ave a fag.

SCRAWDYKE: Oh—ta.

(*Pause.*)

ANN: I saw you on Monday night.

SCRAWDYKE: Where?

ANN: Walkin' past t' Co-op.

SCRAWDYKE: Oh.

ANN: I was waitin' for t' trolley.

SCRAWDYKE: Oh, well. A didn't see y'.

ANN: A thought y' might 'ave done.

SCRAWDYKE: No, no, A didn't.

ANN: A thought it was funny——

SCRAWDYKE: A didn't see y'.

ANN: —A mean if y'd seen me——

SCRAWDYKE: A didn't.

ANN: —y'd 'ave stopped.

SCRAWDYKE: Oh yeh, yeh, if A'd seen y'.

ANN: But y' didn't?

SCRAWDYKE: No A didn't.

ANN: 'S funny A thought for a moment y' 'ad.

SCRAWDYKE: No A didn't.

ANN: Y' just seemed to look in my direction.

SCRAWDYKE: Well A didn't.

121

ANN: A realize that now.

SCRAWDYKE: No I didn't see y'. I was in an 'urry.

ANN: Oh well it's just one o' those things. Where are the others?

SCRAWDYKE: Oh—er—they're out on a mission.

ANN: Connected with the——?

SCRAWDYKE: Yes.

ANN: Oh. A thought A saw 'em goin' int' t' Gates.

SCRAWDYKE: Well—that's where they 'ave t' make a contact.

ANN: Ah. Y're still goin' t' do it then?

SCRAWDYKE: Of course we are.

ANN: An' y're still sure it'll succeed?

SCRAWDYKE: It can't fail.

ANN: It's tomorra night?

SCRAWDYKE: Yes. Ey you 'aven't?

ANN: 'Course not.

SCRAWDYKE: We can't be too careful. We move with stealth.

ANN: That fire doesn't give much off.

SCRAWDYKE: I don't notice the cold.

ANN: 'S just as well.
(*Pause.*)
'Ow would you like t' shaft me?

SCRAWDYKE: Eh!

ANN: I said 'ow would you like to shaft me.

SCRAWDYKE: Buh——!

ANN: It's a simple enough question. 'Ow would you like t' 'ave sexual intercourse with me?
(SCRAWDYKE *is speechless.*)
Either y' would or y' wouldn't.

SCRAWDYKE: I—I—I——

ANN: I don't see any difficulties. It seems quite straightforward t' me. I thought y' prided y'self on y'r rapid perception.

122

SCRAWDYKE: I've never 'eard——

ANN: I know that. That's why A asked y'.

SCRAWDYKE: I don't know 'ow y' dare ask such a question.

ANN: I dare becos there's not the slightest chance of it ever 'appenin'.

SCRAWDYKE: Y' don't just—just—it's disgustin'.

ANN: What's disgustin' about it?

SCRAWDYKE: Well it's a—it's a——

ANN: An' you're the man 'oo prides 'imself on 'is brutal frankness!

SCRAWDYKE: I'm frank when I need t' be. It's all a question of context.

ANN: It's all a question of whether it's Malcolm Scrawdyke 'oo's bein' frank or somebody else.

SCRAWDYKE: I'd never say what you've just said to any woman.

ANN: Only becos y'd never dare.

SCRAWDYKE: Becos I've got a—I've got a proper sense of propriety.

ANN: Well this's a role I never expected. Don't tell me the's a Victorian gentleman lurking beneath all that angry young muck.

SCRAWDYKE: Nobody speaks t' me like——

ANN: That's the trouble. Nobody dare. Y've got the biggest front—I wouldn't 'ave dared either if A 'adn't seen what there is be'ind it. There I was for months in awe of y', just like all t' rest, not darin' t' so much as ask y' what time it was. Dreamin' about the day when the great man might stoop down from 'is 'ights an' deign t' speak t' me. Huh, t' think I used t' think you must 'ave a diff'rent woman ev'ry night o' t' week if y' wanted to. I asked about y', never mind

123

'oo, an' nobody knew anything about it.
So I could only think y' weren't int'rested
or none o' t' women in 'Uddersfield came
up t' y're demands. An' so A screwed up
courage. I screwed up my nerve t' ask you!
An' when y' grunted, when y' grunted
"Yeh" A couldn't believe it, A thought y'
must be puttin' on an act for my benefit. So
we went out an' I was—well, surprised at
first. Then I thought, well 'e's a bit shy,
'e's not used to it after all, so I'll 'elp 'im
along a bit. A bit! An' then I realized the
big secret. The great man's scared stiff of
anything in knickers! Y're the biggest
virgin outside a convent. Y're right, girls
don't usually talk like this. They don't
need to. I don't make an 'abit of it. But
the's no future in being subtle with you.

SCRAWDYKE: The 'ole thing's just a vast misconception
on your part.

ANN: Is it!

SCRAWDYKE: Yes it is. I never looked twice in the way
you mean. I never looked twice at y'.

ANN: That's true, y' didn't even dare look.

SCRAWDYKE: I didn't want to.

ANN: Then why did y' go out with me?

SCRAWDYKE: I'm gregarious.

ANN: An' what were y' doin' 'angin' about down
near our 'ouse?

SCRAWDYKE: I told y'——

ANN: Oh A know what y' told me. An' what
were y' doin' 'angin' around my bus stop?

SCRAWDYKE: I was just walkin' past.

ANN: A know that's what y' did. I'm talkin'
about what y' wanted t' do.

SCRAWDYKE: 'Ow d' you know what I wanted t' do?

124

ANN: I've got a magic eye 'at sees straight
through little men like you.

SCRAWDYKE: Don't call me a little man.

ANN: In spite of the beard an' long scruffy 'air.

SCRAWDYKE: I don't waste my time on hair!

ANN: It doesn't waste its time on you.

SCRAWDYKE: It grows where it should in the way that it
should. I know what it's up to. I leave it
alone. Show me a well-groomed 'ead and
I'll show you an enemy of the creative
imagination.

ANN: A beautiful thought never came from a
beautiful 'ead. Y're the daftest man A've
ever met.

SCRAWDYKE: I'm not going t' waste my time talkin'
about 'air.

ANN: Y' prefer t' waste y' time in other ways.

SCRAWDYKE: You can't see——

ANN: Never mind what A can't see. Let me tell
y' what A can. I see three timid little men.
One 'oo leads the other two along becos
'e's got a louder voice that's all, an' fills
'em up wi' big ideas of 'emselves. One 'oo's
very quick at ev'rything but standin' up for
'imself. 'E's another great lover. I once
caught cold waiting for 'im t' make a move
in a freezin' yard. And a third—well, 'e's
only ever anywhere becos 'e's not
somewhere else.

(SCRAWDYKE *grins*.)

A see y' recognize these descriptions.

SCRAWDYKE: I 'ave a taste for caricature.

ANN: Well these three supermen are goin' t' pinch
a paintin' from a completely unguarded
art gallery, they're goin' t' sneak up be'ind
a completely unsuspectin' 'eadmaster an'

125

clout 'im over the ead. Then they're goin'
t' blackmail 'im by threatenin' t' expose
the fact that 'e kissed a girl student under
t' mistletoe at a Chris'mas party unless 'e's
prepared t' smash up the paintin' they've
pinched. Then they're goin' t' break their
promise to 'im an' tell ev'rybody what a
rotter he is. Then ev'rybody'll see what
great big 'eroes they all are. This's the
great scheme these three giant brains 'ave
been buildin' up over the last week. But
Allard's worth ten of 'em.

SCRAWDYKE: So that's what y' came up 'ere for. Allard's
worth ten of us is 'e! Well you'll see. Now I
know 'oo's side you're on.

ANN: Oh don't be silly. I've no special love for
Allard. 'E tends t' bully sometimes, an' the
way 'e tried t' ostracize you was very bad,
but 'e's not a bad man, 'e does 'is best.
The thing is, 'e goes the wrong way about
it. A feel rather sorry for 'im really——

SCRAWDYKE: Sorry for 'im! Sorry for that bastard!
That's the last thing y' should be. There
should be no pity for a ruthless, scheming,
maniac like 'im. 'E should be regarded as a
rabid vicious animal, the slightest flicker of
sympathy and 'e'll be at y'r throat. That's
exactly what 'e wants. Pity to 'im is
weakness. 'E 'as no normal 'uman feelings.
'E's a monster. A completely separate
species. A stinking accretion that pollutes
ev'rything merely by its existence. The only
thing t' do with—filth like that, the only
course open, is to hack it to pieces!

ANN: D' y' know 'oo y're talkin' about! D' y'
really know 'oo y're— D' y' know what

y're sayin'?

SCRAWDYKE: I always know exactly what I'm sayin'.

ANN: I 'ope y' don't. For your sake I——

SCRAWDYKE: What d' y' mean for my sake!

ANN: A mean if y' really believe all this twisted—
then there's no 'ope for y'. That's why I
came. Can't y' see what—I mean if y' can't
be stopped——

SCRAWDYKE: Ah stopped! Oh yes. Whatever it is I might
want t' do, I've always got t' be
stopped——

ANN: Oh I don't mean in that way. Can't y' see
y' silly bugger what I— I mean stopped
thinkin' all this, stopped bein' all this. All
this twisted nonsense. All this pretence at
bein' something y're not an' shouldn't ever
want t' be. All this great man stuff 'at
wouldn't be a great man even if it was. A
mean even if y' were it. It's all wrong it's
all sick. A don't know— But I feel y' could
be— Y' must see 'at what A'm sayin' is
true. Y' must know why I came. I came
'ere t' 'elp y'. I came 'ere t' 'elp y'.
(*Pause.*)

SCRAWDYKE: Y' came 'ere t'——
(*Short pause.*)

ANN: Yes.

SCRAWDYKE: Well—'ow—'ow could you——?

ANN: I don't know, Malcolm, it's for you——

SCRAWDYKE: If—er, y' know, if—if——

ANN: Mm.
(*Pause.*)

SCRAWDYKE: Oh no! Listen to you and I'd be finished.
Reduced to a slack mouthed nonentity,
wanderin' about grinnin' at babies, sniffin'
flowers, pattin' dogs on t' 'ead. Well that's

127

not for me. I'm a man of a diff'rent stamp.
When I'm angry I know 'at I'm alive, my
blood runs, I tingle, I am something.
(*Footsteps on the stairs.* WICK *and* INGHAM
come in.)

INGHAM: Oh!

WICK: Aye aye.

ANN: 'Lo.

WICK: What's all this then?

ANN: A'm just goin'.

WICK: Oh— Come up from Tech?

ANN: Yeh. A was just on me way 'ome. A
thought A'd pop in.

WICK: Oh. 'Ow's Tech these days?

ANN: Well— T' 'eatin' wasn't workin' properly
until t'day. But a man came up an' got it
rumblin' an' gurglin'.

WICK: 'T sounds like a train comin' in.

INGHAM: Aye it does.

ANN: Yeh.

INGHAM: A suppose like y' di'n't do Life t' first——

ANN: No we couldn't.

WICK: What d' y' do Costume Life instead?

ANN: Yeh.

SCRAWDYKE: Why don't y' ask 'er 'ow Mr. Allard is?

WICK: Eh?

SCRAWDYKE: She's in the best possible position t' tell y'
'ow y' should care t' know about 'im becos
she came 'ere straight from 'im.

ANN: Oh really even——

WICK: Ey! Is this true?

ANN: Of course it's not!

SCRAWDYKE: All right explain to 'em why y' came. I'll
keep my mouth shut, I'll keep completely
out of it. Never let it be said I tried t'
prejudice y'r position.

128

ANN: You bastard!

SCRAWDYKE: Well that's goin' t' make a fine impression
for a start.

WICK: What y' doin' 'ere?

ANN: Oh—I came t' try an' stop y', stop y'
be'avin' like a bunch o' kids.

WICK: 'Ow d' y' mean?

ANN: Oh come off it Wick.

WICK: No. What d' y' mean?

ANN: All this nonsense y've got cooked up for
tonight——

WICK: 'Ow d' y' know about that?

ANN: 'Ow d' y' think! I was told about it.

WICK: Told! 'Oo told——

ANN: Your great leader 'imself told me.

WICK: Mal?

SCRAWDYKE: 'S quite true. I'll tell y' 'ow it 'appened.
When she came through that door I was
almost surprised. I immediately asked
myself why. I flicked through the
permutations an' I came up with the
answer. She'd been sent as a spy. Why else
should she come 'ere?

ANN: Oh this's—I'm not listenin' to any more.
(*She moves towards the door.*)

SCRAWDYKE: Oh no we can't 'ave that. Straight down t'
report t' Philip David Trevor.
(WICK *moves between* ANN *and door, as yet
unmenacingly.*)

WICK: Yeh. Y' can't just shove off. There are
things t' be explained.

ANN: Oh it's obviously— You two believe
ev'rything this bastard wants y' t' believe.
Talk about suckers! I'm not goin' t'
bother——
(*She moves again towards the door.* WICK

129

blocks her way.)

WICK: So we're suckers are we?

ANN: Let me pass.

(SCRAWDYKE *moves beside* WICK.)

SCRAWDYKE: Oh no. She thinks we're goin' t' let 'er run out of 'ere, just like that.

WICK: If we did then we should be suckers.

ANN: Get out of the way y' silly——

SCRAWDYKE: We're only silly kids. We aren't capable of doin' anything.

WICK: Is that so. Well, we'll 'ave t' try an' convince 'er otherwise.

(ANN *moves forward, she makes a gesture to push* WICK *out of the way, he gently pushes her off.*)

P'raps this'll convince 'er.

ANN: Now look, don't be——

SCRAWDYKE: It's beginnin' t' dawn. P'raps we aren't playin'.

WICK: She's beginnin' t' get a bit anxious.

ANN: Oh don't be ridiculous. Now come——

SCRAWDYKE: She's not sure now. P'raps we aren't just things after all.

(*They start to move towards her, she backs away.*)

ANN: Now look not even you——

SCRAWDYKE: Not even us but she backs away.

WICK: She speaks with contempt but she backs away.

SCRAWDYKE: We aren't men she says but she's a woman.

(ANN *moves farther away as they slowly approach her.*)

WICK: An' she's all alone with us up 'ere.

SCRAWDYKE: Outside the snow muffles all sound.

WICK: There's nobody in the buildin'.

SCRAWDYKE: She's weak an' warm an' frightened.

130

(INGHAM *starts moving towards her too. She continues to back away.*)

ANN: All right, all right, you win, y've scared me, if that's what y' want.

SCRAWDYKE: That's not what we want.

WICK: We want more than that.

SCRAWDYKE: We've got to show 'er what 'appens t' women 'oo pry.

WICK: Show 'er what we can do.

SCRAWDYKE: T' women 'oo treat men with contempt.

ANN: Look, please.

SCRAWDYKE: Ah! She starts to beg.

WICK: She's terrified.

SCRAWDYKE: She's quiverin'.

WICK: She's waitin'.

SCRAWDYKE: For their hands.

WICK: On 'er warm soft body.

SCRAWDYKE: Which must be punished, punished, punished——

ANN: No, no, no, no, y' don't, now stop, please, enough's, no, no—

WICK: Punished, punished, punished——

INGHAM: Punished, punished, punished——

(ANN *is too terrified now to speak. They are almost on her when* SCRAWDYKE *breaks into the dog howls we have heard in earlier scenes. The howls are immediately taken up by the other two. When they are only about a foot from her she suddenly leaps at them and tries to club her way through. She flails her arms and hits with her fists. They pounce on her violently, howling at the top of their voices. She screams. They savagely beat her down. Doubled up and under a rain of blows she tries to escape their frenzy but only manages to get a little way.* INGHAM *seizes at*

131

her and tears her coat half off. A blow from
WICK *across the face sends her reeling back.*
All on top of her they beat her down
relentlessly, she crumples to the ground as
the blows stun her. SCRAWDYKE *kicks her*
prostrate body. Their frenzy abates, the
howling ceases. She lies motionless. They
stand around her exhausted, panting. As they
stand there the realization of what they have
done begins to break through. WICK *totters*
round her.)

WICK: Oh!

(*He kneels down to her, stares, then he pulls*
her face round gently, listens, moves her arm
which is completely limp.)
Ey!— Ey!——

SCRAWDYKE: What——

WICK: Oh!

SCRAWDYKE: Wha's——

WICK: She's dead!

SCRAWDYKE: Eh!

(INGHAM *makes a little moaning sound.*)

WICK: She's dead! We've killed 'er. She's dead!
(*Slowly they draw back from the body. They*
are stunned. SCRAWDYKE *sinks down on to a*
box, crumples and moans. The others watch
him and wait. Then:)

INGHAM: Mal! What—what——

(SCRAWDYKE *is oblivious to their questions.*)

WICK: What are we goin' t' do?— What are we
goin' t' do Mal?
(*Slowly the girl starts to come round. They*
watch her, transfixed with horror. She
dazedly stumbles to her feet, looks around
wild-eyed, then retching, staggers across the
room and through the door. We hear her

stumbling down the stairs. Silence.
SCRAWDYKE *pulls himself together.*)

SCRAWDYKE: Tergiversator! The whole thing was feigned.
The whole thing was nothing but another
trick! We ought to 'ave been more
thorough. She ought to 'ave been dead.
She deserved it. You seemed abashed, you
seemed disconsolate. We mustn't be
abashed by things like this. We must steel
ourselves. It's them or us. Remember that.
It's those 'oo strike first. Do you think
she'd 'ave 'esitated for a minute, for a
second, if she'd been the stronger? Oh no!
I know 'ow y' felt lads, the first time.
We're too humane that's our trouble, it
does us credit. I had a suspicion all along
that she was feigning. But I didn't let on.
Do you know why? I'll tell you why.
There's a streak of weakness, of
sentimentality, in all of us. It's got to be
recognized, it's got to be wrestled with. It's
got to be brought out into the open. It
needs the right incident to entice it out. I
used this incident. I let it come out. I gave
it full play. I let it suffuse me. So that once
and for all time, with utter finality, I could
reject it. That's the way to handle
temptations. Every saint knew that, let 'em
roll then smack 'em down. Well I smacked
mine down. I was just on the verge of
giving mine the chop when she shoved off.
Another second and I was going t' say:
"Hack up the body." Never mind, there'll
be other opportunities. What we've just
done makes the putsch even more urgent.
If we don't act decisively now our

133

destruction of her threat will have been in vain. We shall have done it all for nothing. Have we been through so much, suffered such privations, been goaded to such extremities for nothing? We most certainly have not. We are about to leap from our corner at the throat of the world! And then we shall see who cries for mercy, and then we shall see who begs for it, and then we shall see who gets it! We are the Arbiters of the Future!

(*Short pause.*)

WICK: Yeh, well, we'd better get ready.

INGHAM: Aye A suppose so.

(*He gets the portfolio.*)

SCRAWDYKE: When the time comes, Act, Act, don't think, Act.

INGHAM: 'Ow long is there t' go?

(SCRAWDYKE *is now standing still.*)

SCRAWDYKE: One minute.

WICK: Well this is it.

INGHAM: Seemin'ly so.

(*He puts the portfolio under his arm.*)

WICK: I avn't made a will.

SCRAWDYKE: Thirty seconds—twenty—fifteen—five—one.

(SCRAWDYKE *stands where he is. The others stand where they are, watching him, absolutely motionless. The pause must be held for as long as possible. Then suddenly—*)

WICK: We're not goin' t' do it! We're not goin' t' do it! After all the noise from 'im, after what 'e's just made us do t' that bird, after what 'e's just said, when the moment arrives 'e 'asn't got the nerve t' do it. Look at 'im—like a bloody statue! Petrified! Oh

134

this's the biggest come down I've ever—
Oh after all the crap! We're ready t' foller
'im through that door. All we're waitin' for
is 'is say so. An' 'e can't make it! The 'ole
bloody thing was wind! The Great Leader,
that miserable lump of solidified crap
transfixed there!

(SCRAWDYKE *moves.*)

SCRAWDYKE: So I couldn't——

WICK: All this for nothing! Well this's the end.

SCRAWDYKE: Well I didn't notice you jumpin' into
action.

WICK: I was waitin' for you. You were the Great
Leader.

SCRAWDYKE: Yeh waitin' for me as always.

WICK: It was all y'r idea. You made us!

SCRAWDYKE: With what—a gun?

WICK: With y' bloody words. With all y' lies.
Well y're spell's broken. An' I'm goin' t'
make sure it stays that way.

SCRAWDYKE: Ah y're goin' t' kill me.

WICK: I'm goin' t' tell people what you are. Then
they'll know!

SCRAWDYKE: I know you.

WICK: I'm gettin' out o' this freezin' 'ole. I'm off
through that door an' A'm not comin'
back. You bastard y've ruined my life!

SCRAWDYKE: Well at least I've achieved something.

WICK: Nobody's listenin'. Come on, Irwin.

(INGHAM *shakes his head.*)

Y're not stayin' 'ere after—

(INGHAM *shrugs.*)

Aargh y' must be——

SCRAWDYKE: Go on crawl away——

WICK: Nobody's listenin'.

135

(*He goes out, slams door. His feet are heard running down the stairs.*)

SCRAWDYKE: What a turd! Good riddance! I ought to 'ave known better than to— Well you 'aven't said owt as usual. I know what y' think. Go on say it, y' might as well.

INGHAM: Well, Mal—A don't think as 'ow we can put it all on t' you. A don't think 'at what John said— We di'n't 'ave t' go along like, we di'n't 'ave to listen. A mean if we're goin' t' start talkin' about 'oo's to blame, 'oo's the worst one like, y' know, well A reckon, A reckon as y' could say I was, I am. A mean whereas you an' Wick, like, seemed t' 'ave, well—some genuine belief like, in what we were goin' t' do an' 'ow feasible it might be, well, y' see, I never did. I knew all along, like, from when y' suggested it, as 'ow it couldn't really work, an' as 'ow—well, y'd invented a lot of it. A mean A know y'— But anyway A just went on, A kept me mouth shut, A joined in— So really, y' could say like, 'at I'm the one 'oo——

SCRAWDYKE: Nah. I instigated it. I'm not goin' t'— Anyway y're 'onest Irwin. 'Ere 'ave a fag.

INGHAM: Ta.

SCRAWDYKE: Just three left. That's all we got t' show for t' 'ole campaign. Three fags.

INGHAM: Well——

SCRAWDYKE: Aargh if only I'd 'ad the nerve!

INGHAM: No—it was a good thing y' couldn't.

SCRAWDYKE: P'raps y're right. P'raps it wasn't just a failure of nerve. P'raps it was some kind of warning message sent up from me subconscious. Some kind of switch thrown

136

down there t' stop me. An inner sense of
realism stepped in at the last moment and
struck me rigid. I knew all along the thing
wasn't feasible but I got carried away,
pinned ev'rything to it, papered over the
cracks. Lookin' back I can see all the
mistakes. I should never 'ave tried t' use
people like Wick an' Nipple. Inferior
material. I shouldn't 'ave tried t' do it so
quickly, I should 'ave got funds, got
backin', got organs. Listen Irwin, it's you
an' me now. Let's pack this town in, get
out, there's nothing 'ere. Let's get down
London. That's where it all is. That's
where they all are, millions of 'em. All the
dissatisfied, waitin'. We can start all over
again, right from scratch. We'll get jobs,
build up some money, build up the 'ole
thing slowly, meet people. I know you
didn't agree with the old aims, well we'll
work out new ones, a completely new set,
together. We'll 'ammer 'em out as equals,
y' can 'ave a veto, we'll be joint Leaders. If
I open my big trap too much y' can tell me
t' shut it. I won't speak without your
permission. It'll be you an' me——

INGHAM: No! Mal, no.

SCRAWDYKE: But what is there 'ere for you! Crawl back
to Allard. 'E won't 'ave y' back. An' what's
left? Some mis'rable job—tintin' snapshots.

INGHAM: Well if that's what it is that's what it'll 'ave
t' be. It's no good Mal, A know y' too
well. An' it's not just that, even if
ev'rything y' say could— Well A'm not cut
out for it.

SCRAWDYKE: Well——

137

INGHAM: All this power stuff. A mean even if I 'ave
'ad—certain—at times— Well A don't
think like I ought to 'ave——

SCRAWDYKE: Oh I know what y' mean. Y' think 'at
certain things we did were—wrong. Even
bad. Well there is something in——

INGHAM: It's no use, Mal, whatever y' say. A'm not
'avin' owt else t' do wi' parties an'
movements an' erections, whatever y' say.

SCRAWDYKE: The answer's no?

INGHAM: The answer's no.

SCRAWDYKE: So after twenty-five years y've finally made
a decision.

INGHAM: It seems so.

SCRAWDYKE: I never thought I'd live t' see it.

INGHAM: Come t' that, nor did I.

SCRAWDYKE: Well—well—good for you. Well go on then,
piss off if that's what y' want.

INGHAM: Oh well just becos A'm not joinin' any
more movements doesn't mean like——

SCRAWDYKE: We can't remain friends.

INGHAM: Aye.

SCRAWDYKE: That's no use t' me. Y're runnin' out on
me like all the rest.

INGHAM: No A'm not.

SCRAWDYKE: 'Course you are. So get on with it!

INGHAM: Well if that's—
(*Pause.*)
What y' goin' t' do?

SCRAWDYKE: Mind y're own business!

INGHAM: The's no need t' be like that. No, A mean
seriously, what a' y' goin' t' do?

SCRAWDYKE: What the 'ell d' y' think A'm goin' to do?

INGHAM: Well, A suppose mebbe go down London.

SCRAWDYKE: Go down London. A lot o' good that's
goin' t' do me.

138

INGHAM: Y' just said——

SCRAWDYKE: If the's one thing I can do without it's somebody t' tell me what I've just said.

INGHAM: Well what'll y' do then?

SCRAWDYKE: What can I do?

INGHAM: Mebbe tek a job?

SCRAWDYKE: I've never done an honest day's work in me life an' I don't intend t' start now.

INGHAM: Well if y' don't, A mean, what——

SCRAWDYKE: What can I do? There isn't anything I can do. I've no way to turn. I'm a complete and utter failure. I can't do anything, I've no resources. I'm finished. There's only one logical endin' t' this 'ole idiotic drama.

INGHAM: What's that?

SCRAWDYKE: What do y' think it is? If I've nothing t' live for.

INGHAM: Oh don't talk like that. A mean even if y' don't mean it don't talk like that.

SCRAWDYKE: When life becomes completely meaningless an' y' can't move in any direction.

INGHAM: Oh if y' really mean it y' wouldn't talk about it.

SCRAWDYKE: I talk about ev'rything.

INGHAM: If A thought y' really meant it A'd stay like, A mean for t'night.

SCRAWDYKE: Oh no, y' won't, go on get out.

INGHAM: Well——

SCRAWDYKE: Go on!

INGHAM: Right. A'll just get me sleepin'-bag. (*He goes and gets it, rolls it up.*) Er, look Mal.

SCRAWDYKE: Get out! Tek y' bag an' piss off! (INGHAM *finishes tucking up his sleeping-bag and goes out. The door closes. His feet plod down the stairs. Silence.*)

139

Well that's it. The last of 'em gone. 'Ere I
am, alone, empty, nothing! If only I— Oh!
I'm not a person, I don't amount— I can't
function on any level. They'll all be all
right, they all live lives of their own in
some way. As Irwin trudges 'ome through
t' snow 'e is something, 'e 'as authenticity.
'E'll go on, get a menial job, find a bird,
get married, 'owever inadequate 'e'll keep
goin', 'e'll 'ave an identity. Wick, well at
least 'e's a painter, 'e 'as that, 'e'll crawl
back down t' Allard, justify it becos of 'is
talent, laugh an' joke, 'ide 'is weakness, an'
generally get on with some kind of a living.
Nipple, even Nipple 'as 'is fantasies, they're
real fantasies, 'e believes in 'em, they give
'im something, they are 'im. 'E'll go on,
self-contained, dreamin', talkin'. I can't
even believe in my own fantasies! They'll
all go on. Allard, Boocock, all the rest,
they'll all get on with it. Except me! Except
me! Oh I can't stand it. This! Ev'rything
exists except me, ev'rything 'as an identity.
These objects, these easels, these cups, this
dustbin, they all flaunt me! There's only
one logical—as I told Irwin. That's the
obvious—no doubt about that. But I
couldn't even— But if I could. If there was
a simple, quick— 'Ow could I do it? 'Ow
could I? Gas? Well that's out for a start.
Poison? Painless no violence. What could I
poison meself with? Paint, squeeze a tube
down me throat? Ugh no! Old tea leaves.
Tannin? No just give y' cramps. Swaller a
lump o' wood? Mouldy bread? We 'aven't
any. Suck the dye out of me coat? Fluff?

Fluff kills cats. Nah!— Smother y'self? Put
y'r 'ead under a pillow an' press. No that's
not a do-it-yourself method, y've got t' 'ave
pressure. Put y'r 'ead through t' doorway
and pull it shut. Snap? Oh don't be— I
could throw meself out o' t' winder.
(*Goes to window.*)
Aaar can't get it open. Too small t' get
through anyway. 'Ang meself. From what?
Aaargh this place isn't designed for suicide.
Go out. Under a bus? They move too
slowly in this— Bury y'self in a drift? No
no it's got t' be quick, no pre-
determination. A knife?
(*Rummages about.*)
Where— We 'ad a knife— What's this? A
spoon! All we've got are spoons. Y' can't
do away with y'self with a spoon! We 'ad
a— 'Ere's a fork. 'T's got prongs, I suppose
they'd go in. All right. Where? Soft part.
Belly. Back. No can't push it in there.
Where's soft an' vital? Buttocks. No
wouldn't even be able to sit down after—
What after? There mustn't be an after.
That's the 'ole bloody— 'Eart! That's it.
Get that. Where is it? Right side? Left
side? Where? Where? Left, yes left. It's
'ard there. Through the ribs that's 'ow they
do it. Feel there. Now get it ready. Close
y're eyes. An'— Ugh!
(*He staggers about gasping and falls to the
floor.*)
Very fittin'! A phoney suicide to end a
phoney drama. A travesty of a death to
finish off a travesty of a life. I'm still 'ere,
I'm still 'ere! Oh I can't stand this silence.

Let's— Music.

(*Jumps up. Goes to tape recorder, switches it on, runs tape back a little, stops it. "Hail Scrawdyke, Hail Scrawdyke—" booms out of it. He stands for a moment then switches it off.*)

Oh what am I goin' t' do! I should 'ave a mental breakdown. That's what this should be. I should collapse, let 'em carry me away. Aar I can't even manage that. Even a mental breakdown needs more willpower than I've got. Why am I like— Oh Ann, she came 'ere to save me, I could 'ave—I could 'ave—what? I know there's another side. A warm dimension. What did we do! What did I— It was the act of animals.— Oogh! I can't stand it. I can't. There's nothing I can do. No way I— Ring Ann up. Apologize! Oh don't be absurd. Of all the things I've ever it's the most impossible. But if I could, I mean how—I mean if——

(*Scrawdyke paces up and down through a rapid and subtle light change which denotes the night passing. When the morning light is growing he sits in his chair. Full morning light. He looks at his watch. He is completely calm, drained, objective.*)

SCRAWDYKE: Nearly ten. Well it's nearly it. I know what I'm going t' do. As soon as it's ten, I'll walk through that door, go down the stairs, walk across the top o' Chapel 'ill, through the snow, go into one o' the kiosks opposite, dial Ann's number. If 'er mother answers I'll ask for 'er. When she comes I'll say:

142

Hallo, this is Malcolm Scrawdyke, please don't ring off. I know how you feel but please listen. I want to apologize. I know that words can't begin to make up for what I did, I'm not trying to excuse it, there is no excuse. I just want you to know that I'm deeply ashamed. No words can express how disgusted I am with myself. I'm not asking you to forgive me. What I did was unforgivable. I don't even expect you to believe me. I simply wanted to try and tell you that I shall never forgive myself.

(*He gets up and goes to window.*)

Right. The kiosk's empty.

(*Looks at watch.*)

Fifteen—ten—five—two— Right.

(*He walks across the room, goes through the door, closes it behind him. His footsteps are heard going down the stairs. Silence. The light slowly fades out on the empty room.*)

THE END